The Miller's Boy

BARBARA WILLARD
The Miller's Boy

illustrated by Gareth Floyd

E. P. Dutton & Co., Inc.   New York

REMEMBERING T. L.

Summer of '75

First published in the U.S.A. 1976 by E. P. Dutton
Text copyright © 1976 by Barbara Willard
Illustrations copyright © 1976 by Gareth Floyd

Library of Congress Cataloging in Publication Data

Willard, Barbara   The miller's boy

SUMMARY: In fifteenth-century Sussex a young boy
living with his grandfather, a harsh miller, dreams of
having a friend his age and a horse to take him to his
married sister.

[1. England—Social life and customs—Medieval period,
1066-1485—Fiction]   I. Floyd, Gareth   II. Title

PZ7.W6547Mi3   [Fic]   76-19058   ISBN 0-525-34970-7

Printed in the U.S.A.   First Edition
10 9 8 7 6 5 4 3 2 1

Contents

1. Boy Alone

Thomas could tell, almost before he was awake, what
sort of day it was likely to be. What sort of weather;
therefore, what sort of work. His bed was in the kitchen
– warm in winter, when the embers glowed on after the
end of the day, stifling in summer. It was summer now.
In the wall across the room from Thomas's bed was a
small window. It showed him a fair section of the mill,
standing a hundred paces or so from the house; it let
in the sound of wind tugging at the sails and promising
hard work ahead, and of rain lashing against the wooden
body of the mill; it let in the quiet of such a morning
as this one, breathless, no stir, no sound, even, for the
birds had stopped their morning song as the cares of
parenthood overtook them. There would be no milling
today, and though that might not mean a holiday for
Thomas, yet it meant the hardest work was at a stand-
still.

Thomas stretched out in bed curling and uncurling
his toes. There might be some task about the forest for
him, and that could only please him.

He heard a sound on the rickety stairway and leapt
from his bed. His older sister, Agnes, who kept house

for the pair of them and their grandfather, came yawning into the kitchen, still in her petticoat, barefooted, and braiding her hair as she came.

'You slept all night wi' that window gaping!' she cried.

'What of it? There's none'll come and clim over the sill.'

'Fever and ague come climming, brother Thomas. How often do I say it?'

She said it very often indeed. Agnes was a great one for fever and ague – when he was small Thomas had quite thought they were twin monsters, which might indeed come crawling and climbing into the house at night. He grinned at his sister's sleepy face as she bent to blow the fire. Agnes was twelve years older than Thomas – which meant that this year he would be half her age. He loved her very warmly – but his true affection lay with his second sister, Betsy, who had married and left them, going far away, right to the other side of London. A five days' journey, someone had told them.

'No wind,' said Agnes. 'The fire won't draw. Open the door, Thomas.' She sat back on her heels and looked out as he swung the heavy old door. 'A very fair day, brother.'

'Gaffer'll never say so.' Thomas pulled a long face at the thought of his grandfather's stamping and raging; he could hardly be called a patient man.

'We'll all grow old and full of crotchets,' Agnes

8

said. 'Get your clothes on. Have you said your prayers?'

'I barely woke yet!'

'The Almighty don't reckon much of being kept waiting, Thomas Welfare.'

Thomas dashed outside, stuffing his shirt into the top of his shabby hose and carrying his doublet in his teeth. There was a half pail of water standing on the well rim. He struggled into the doublet – an old one of his grandfather's with the sleeves cut out – then plunged both hands into the pail, threw some of the water over his head and sleeked at his hair, drank a mouthful or two from the dipper, and then sprang up the wooden steps and into the mill. He preferred to say his prayers on the top floor of the mill, kneeling by the window there, with all the forest spread beneath him. Although his two most important requests gave no sign of being attended to, he did feel it ought to help if he sped them on their way from such a point – a step at least nearer to the ear of God, waiting at that hour, no doubt, to collect the morning petitions of all humble enough to make them.

'First, a horse, Lord,' said Thomas as usual. 'Any old nag shall do – so be he's life enough to carry me where my sister Betsy live now wi' her husband. And best there be a saddle for that long ride.' He spoke these words out loud, in faith, hope and a great resolution to be patient. He waited a bit, as if to let one request on its way before making another. His second prayer was a silent one. He prayed without words for the souls of his mother and father, then he went on. 'Jesu,' he said urgently, 'if not the horse, then let some other lads come settling in these parts. So I may have a friend to myself, to fish and chase with. And keep me from sin this day, and let me be forgive for what I do wrong, days before this one. Amen. Mother Mary, see my prayer safe. Amen.'

He crossed himself and the day began.

Thomas stayed on by the window, looking out between the silent, motionless sails. In the early summer morning, the stillness could be heard and felt. A high pale sky had sucked up the larks that had returned now to their singing, and the notes came faint and formless. There was a fuzz of mist across the distance, blurring the far horizon. The mill itself was tall, and it was set on a mound of its own, and that again at the top of a hill. Thomas's grandfather always said that if a mill might be made tall enough there need never be a day with too little wind to swing the sweeps. But then it would be so high, he reckoned it must either topple or break in two. Anyone knew that Miller Welfare was halfway mad – he sometimes spoke of mills with six sails, eight sails. Mad or no, he was not only Thomas's grandfather but his master, and had all the ordering of his life.

'I'll be off any day, see if I'm not,' Thomas would cry to Agnes. 'I'll get me a horse and be off to Betsy and Saul and work for'm. I'll make a fair farmer – better'n ever a miller's boy.'

'You've more sisters than just the one,' Agnes would reproach him.

'You'll be marrying wi' Miles Hoad.'

'Maybe so, maybe not. . . And we'll never see you set up any higher nor faster than a donkey! No need to scowl – better men than you rid a donkey afore now, Thomas Welfare.'

Betsy would not call him *Thomas Welfare*, so sternly, but *Tom* or *Tomkin*. He had never been lonely while Betsy was at home, nor missed the brother who had died as soon as born, taking their mother away with him. He'd be nine years old now, sharing the days, roaming the forest with Thomas for his hero; ready to do battle against those lads who came carting their fathers' grain for milling, their sisters tagging along, and shouted names at Thomas – *Miller's mawkin, Gaffer's nidget*; and others far worse. . .

A door slammed and a voice shouted, bellowed: '*Thomas!*'

Thomas looked down from the top of the windmill. He saw his grandfather coming from the house, with its perpetual dusting of wind-blown flour, slamming the fore-door behind him, shouting as he came.

'Thomas! *Thomas!*'

From up above, as he came snudging towards the mill, he looked a very small old man. Thomas, who often felt he might like to knock him flat and stamp on him, experienced an uneasy pang – love or pity, or both. The old man had seemed lately to move more rapidly towards the end of his life. His back was increasingly stooped, a miller's back, bent by sack carrying, pinned by age.

'Thomas!' he roared again, in a voice that quite denied any hint of frailty and immediately released his grandson from that twinge of compassion. 'Thomas – thee ill-conditioned, nunty squab! Come'n I call!'

Thomas leant out and bawled back, knowing well that his grandfather would never distinguish the words – 'Roupy old runagate!'

Then he turned away from his look-out and slid down through the core of the mill in his own particular and particularly dangerous way. His day had begun as he concluded his prayers; his day's work began now.

'No milling today, gaffer,' Thomas said, when he reached his grandfather's side.

'Tuesday,' was the prompt reply. 'Niver-iver a good milling day.'

'No wind,' insisted Thomas.

'Bedstone need dressing. Tuesday come a good stone-dressing day.'

'You said Friday last week, surelye.'

'Hold thy gab, young Thomas.' He stood looking up at the mill. 'Bit o' sun suit her,' he said. She was his pride. She worked for him alone. Sometimes he seemed to think that it was he who whistled up a wind for her, and that when there was no wind, it was because he did not choose to whistle – and whistle he would not on a Tuesday; or Thursday, or Friday, as occasion demanded.

Yet in his love for the mill there was also fear, even a touch of hatred. 'She'll be the death o' me yet,' he would say – and indeed the mill had certainly been the death of his only son. It was then that he had tried to call a blessing on the place by naming the four sails Matthew, Mark, Luke, John. Now, all over that countryside, Welfare's mill was known as Gospels Mill.

It was when a strong, stormy wind blew that Miller Welfare seemed most mad. Then the sails tore round, carving the sky into rags, setting wheels and cogs and pulleys whining and rumbling, violently shaking the mill's wooden body that felt at such times as frail as tinder. 'Hark how she do battle!' the old man would cry then. And shouting out to her, 'My beauty! My beauty!' he would slap at the wooden walls as if encouraging and urging on some great beast of burden struggling with storm and tempest to do its master's bidding.

Such times made Thomas shiver with fright, and for nights after he might dream of what millers most dread – of the wind so strong the brake could not hold the sails, of the brake snatching and binding until sparks flew, flame leapt and fire consumed all. . .

'Matthew need her canvas stitching,' Miller Welfare said this Tuesday morning, standing with his hands on his hips, gazing up at the still and silent sweeps. He never said *he* or *his* of things, only of people.

'Agnes did make a sound patch for Luke,' said Thomas. 'She'll do samely for Matthew.'

'Your sister's a good kind of wretch,' old Welfare

13

said. 'She know where her duty lie – not like that Betsy, jigging off pillion behind a husband she'd barely wed but an hour or two.'

'So where'd a wife's duty lie, then?' Thomas asked, rushing to Betsy's defence.

'And where lie thine, Thomas? Swep' up have 'ee?'

It was Thomas's first job of any day to sweep out dust and chaff, brush over the cogs, and see the mill fair and tidy for the day's work.

'Do it now, gaffer.'

'Quick about it, then. I got two-three sacks need carting.'

Thomas's heart lightened, though his muscles clenched instinctively. He sometimes hauled meal sacks for what seemed leagues across the forest.

'Where to, gaffer?'

'Over Ghylls Hatch. Mus' Orlebar need 'em. Three mares foaling and short on bran – so he tell by Peter Crutten who pass this way. Sweep up clean, then get you off, boy. Best load up the donkey – a fair step, here to there.'

Now indeed Thomas's spirits skipped with pleasure. So fine a day, a chance to walk slowly through the sunny morning and look about him as he went – and to think, to plan his escape to Betsy, to wonder where he might come by a horse; for though they were bred by the score at Ghylls Hatch, they were not bred for the likes of Thomas Welfare.

The donkey was in the field next the mill and had

different ideas from Thomas's as to how he should spend his day. It took half an hour and several wisps of new hay to wheedle him into a bridle and get the sacks tidy across his back. For all that, the summer sun was no more than comfortably climbing and noon was far away, as Thomas led out the loaded beast and moved off down the track from the mill. It was a fairly steep way down just here, for Welfare had chosen carefully when first he set up his mill. The best point for miles around, he always boasted. So it had been, then. But there was another good rise some way to the north-west. It had not been available at the time Gospels was being built, for its crown and slopes had been thickly covered with beechwood. Now much of the wood had been felled, in order to meet the demand for timber that could be fed as charcoal into the iron smelting furnaces of the area.

At the head of the track running from Gospels Mill there was an ancient milepost, its figures worn and mossy and impossible to read. The Romans left it, someone had been told; the Romans measured in miles. No one Thomas knew was wise enough to explain what this might mean, and what such *Romans* could have been – giants? wizards? fairies? – yet the stone was looked upon as being in some way important. One or another about the forest would be sure to cut back the brakes and undergrowth and leave it standing clear, as it had stood for as long as anyone living could remember. One day, quite a way further along the track, Thomas had chanced on a second stone. He told no one, but hid it again under its covering of grass and bracken. He feared it, somehow, as he might the footprint of a sorcerer. When he passed it, he looked away. He had to pass it quite often, for it was the halfway mark between his home and Ghylls Hatch. Also, the track branched here, leading off to the right into the bottom, then up

again to another great house whose chimneys could just be seen from the mill. It was a newish house, built perhaps a few years before Thomas was born, on the site of a much older dwelling. There, also, he was sometimes sent.

This was a lonely part of the forest. Though many tracks led to the mill, only the two ran this way. Thomas was well accustomed to the stillness. What movement there was he knew to be the movement of bird and animal, familiar neighbours whose names had somehow always been in his head.

'My mother did learn me,' he told Miles Hoad one day.

'Agnes tell me your mother die when you was only two-year. And do you remember?'

Miles was laughing a little, but very gently. He was a kind and gentle person. Truly Thomas could not recall his mother's face, nor her voice, nor the colour of her hair. He remembered only the loss of her and the names he was so sure she had taught him – hare and stoat, yaffle, badger, scutty-wren, green lintie, nettlecreeper, effet, blind-adder. . . Each time the words came into his mind he thought of her without knowing that he did so. He thought more actively of the lost brother; for him the mourning might never end.

Ahead of Thomas now, as he urged the laden donkey on, he saw the clustered buildings of Ghylls Hatch, and all the great open pasture, won from the rough forest, where the horses grazed. Numberless beasts, and of many kinds – bred for working, bred for riding and hunting; or bred for war and jousting, broad and heavy and deep chested, fit to carry men in armour. So many horses, and never one that Thomas might hope to call his own. The donkey saw them, too, and being, like Thomas, solitary of his kind, without companions, lifted his lip off his great yellow teeth, and flung up his head to give forth his own blood-curdling cry of greeting. He quickened his steps, his hard little hooves pattering on the summer-baked ground, for, from some-where about the place, another donkey had answered.

'It's well for you, beast,' said Thomas, thumping him on the rump. 'What if I shout out? There's no other boy'll shout back.'

Then he jerked at the donkey and checked him. He stood very still under the trees that moved in just here to line the track and shade it. He was fifty paces or so short of the deer pale, looking directly up hill towards Ghylls Hatch. There was a boy ahead of him. He was walking slowly, unwillingly perhaps, towards the con-fusion of stables and barns that stood about this south-eastern quarter of the estate. Near to Thomas's age, surely, since near to Thomas's size. A boy, like him, who walked alone. . .

And now the day changed. It was still Tuesday, still early June, still the year 1478, with England quiet enough, though the old quarrels between York and Lancaster remained unhealed. It was still windless, still no day for milling – but it was also the day on which Thomas Welfare found a friend.

2. Another Boy

Ahead of Thomas, the stranger vanished. He had moved out of sunlight into the shadow of trees that tunnelled upward, gradually obscuring the buildings above. Thomas, excited beyond reason, felt sure he knew where the boy would emerge. He urged on the laden donkey, adding his own weight, pushing and shoving him up the steep little track. The last stretch up to Ghylls Hatch was always hard, even without sacks of bran to carry, and boy and donkey both panted and sweated in the breathlessness of the morning. When they reached the top and went through the gate into the wide yard before the stable area, the boy after all had vanished. . . Perhaps he had never existed, Thomas thought gloomily, but was no more than a trick of light and shade and longing.

Master Roger Orlebar, the owner of Ghylls Hatch, was crossing the yard as Thomas reached it. Orlebar was a short, sturdy man, dark-haired, with a square beard cut close. He called out cheerfully as he came, 'Goodmorrow to you, Thomas Welfare,' though most of his sort would have waited for the boy to pull his forelock before acknowledging him.

'Good-day, Mus' Orlebar. Gaffer sent me wi' your sacks o' chizzle.'

'He ever does keep his word, does your old gaffer.'

Thomas grinned back at him, pleased with the praise. Master Orlebar, a man known to be shy with his own sort of gentry or with any kind of blustering fellows, was easy with animals, children, his own workers and his sister, Jenufer – who was a shade unsteady in her mind.

'Take the donkey, Will,' he said to one of his men who had come up at the sound of voices. 'Come with me, young Thomas. I've a sight to show you.'

He led the way across the yard and into the nearest stable. There stood his bay mare, Dido, among stained and trampled straw, her long neck bent, her great tongue cleaning and caressing the youngest foal Thomas had yet seen.

'She slipped him n'more than half an hour since,' Master Orlebar said. 'The pretty creature. The dear, good girl. What should we name him? He was sired by Perseus. You remember him?'

Thomas nodded. He was struck silent – by the sight of that damp, folded creature, by the tenderness of its mother, by Master Orlebar's friendly manner. As he watched, the foal staggered to its feet and stood swaying, then groped towards its mother, stumbled, righted itself, began to suck. The mare shivered and was still, contentment rippling over her from mane to tail. Even though he was not looking at the spirited four- or five-year-old of which he so often dreamt, Thomas thought the foal the most beautiful young creature he had ever seen.

'Choose me his name,' insisted Master Orlebar, smiling as if he enjoyed the wonder on the boy's face.

Thomas shook his head. He could only think of single words – gentle, soft, fair, loving. He knew that the foal must have a name that could be found in a book, like all the rest of Ghylls Hatch. As he had never been taught to read or write he was at a disavantage. . . Then he did think of one strange word.

'R– Roman?' he asked, red with shyness, and closing his eyes as he waited for Master Orlebar's laugh.

The laugh did not come. 'Roman. Roman. . . Where did you come by the name?'

'Sir, they say the stone – the great stone wi' figures by the trackhead – they do say that got left by Romans. Only – if so be they're evil things, then I'm sorry for saying it.'

'It is a good name, Thomas. Very good. I like it.'

There had been some slight movement behind them. Master Orlebar glanced back and said, as quietly as if to some suspicious animal poised for flight – 'Lewis, we are choosing a name for Dido's foal.'

The boy Thomas had seen vaguely on the shadowy track was still standing back a little in the shadows. Thomas's heart sank. The prayer was answered, but not in one important respect. He should have specified that he needed a lad of his own sort. This one was a gentle-man's son.

'Here's Thomas Welfare from the mill, Lewis. Much of your years, I think... Lewis Mallory is my kinsman, Thomas. He has been made my ward. He'll be living with us here at Ghylls Hatch from now on.'

The boy said nothing. He eyed Thomas slowly and Thomas stood up to the eyeing, telling himself it was nothing that his old doublet, worn very thin in places, was lightened by flour across the shoulders and darkened by many years' sweat under the arms; or that his fair hair hung low in his eyes, because Agnes had had no time lately to take her shears and cut it short and straight; that as well as being bare his legs and feet were also dirty, dust silting up between the toes, right across the instep and up the ankle to mid-shin. He stared back at Lewis, taking in slowly and gloomily the clean shirt, the neatly laced doublet, the good hose and soft boots. Master Orlebar, though a countryman in every neces-sary particular, was yet known to have high and haughty relations.

Yet as he gave back glance for glance, Thomas knew as certainly as if great wisdom were suddenly dropped on him from heaven, that what he and this lad shared – their boyhood – was stronger than any difference between them.

'Thomas has a name for the foal, cousin. But do you choose also, and let me set them one agin the other.'

Still Lewis did not answer, nor smile at Thomas, nor

frown. He looked at him instead with eyes that seemed to darken his whole face. *He has been made my ward*, Master Orlebar had said. Such things could happen to the children of gentlefolk – they might be put into wardship for the profit of one party or another. So it must be with this young stranger, looking so unsuited to a country household – and a household poorly kept, since Master Orlebar had no wife to see the place well cared-for, but only his poor weak-witted sister.

'Thomas says *Roman* could be a good name, Lewis.'

The stranger stirred at the challenge and said shortly: 'Phoebus.'

'Greek against Roman, then! Do you know who Phoebus was, Thomas? I daresay not. Tell him, Lewis.'

Lewis looked briefly at Thomas, looked away, and did not answer.

'Phoebus was the sun god,' Roger Orlebar said to Thomas, who could not imagine what he was talking about. 'It tells in old books how he rode his chariot across the heavens from east to west, giving light and dark to the world. This was heathen thinking, see you. We know better.'

A glance flicked between the two boys. Master Orlebar, for all his goodness and kindness and vigorous manners, did sound just then like every lad's idea of a schoolmaster. Then, as if even that had given too much away, Lewis left the stable.

'His life has turned face-about,' Roger Orlebar said,

more to himself than to Thomas. 'We'll have much of a skirmish, setting it to rights.'

Thomas said timidly, 'Is he – is Master Lewis an orphan, sir?'

'Aye, he is most surely orphaned – though his parents have not died. . . This will sound a mystery, and boys, I recall, love mysteries. But you shall never question him on the matter.'

'No, sir,' said Thomas; it seemed unlikely he would have the chance.

'He must forget what's past and settle with us here. He's young enough. His father knows what's best for him, no doubt. Children are bound to obey. We must help him when he seems homesick. Bear that in mind.'

Thomas did not know what to answer. His first pleasure in coming upon one near to his own age had been dashed by the other boy's style. Yet here was Master Orlebar speaking as if his young kinsman and the miller's boy might still have something to say to one another. It could have seemed more likely had they been a year or two younger. Though they were much of a height, Thomas guessed he was older than Lewis. Even so, Lewis must be into two figures, and so like any other boy at that time leaning towards the cares of life, dreaming of his manhood and seeing his place in the world, whether or not he liked what he saw.

Master Orlebar had turned back to the horses. He ran his hand along Dido's arched neck and spoke a soft word to her. Then he put his hand on the foal, to see if the mare would take exception. She stood easy and trusting.

'We'll call him Roman, then. A good name – though his parents do come of a different order.' He bent to inspect a mark on Dido's right hock, speaking as he did so, throwing in Thomas's direction more strange words. 'Boys need boys, Thomas. You shall be my cousin's *famulus*, as near as daily life allows.'

Bewildered, Thomas frowned and shifted his feet. *Famulus?* It sounded like a word heard in church. It would be some sort of servant, no doubt. If the idea was a vague disappointment after what had gone before, he had no call to find it so. But what might his grandfather say? He was Gaffer's servant already, and it was rightly said no man could serve two masters.

'Do you know what that is – *famulus?*' Master Orlebar asked, straightening up and turning from the horses. 'The young sons of noblemen and the like often have their approved and appointed *famulus*. The son of a trusted family servant, perhaps – but himself more a constant companion – sharing board and bed and lessons and sport. A friend and follower. A whipping boy, most often, to take blame and punishment for the young lord's misdemeanours.'

'I've my own punishments, surelye,' said Thomas, quick and nervous. 'I'll not take another lad's as well, lord or no.'

Master Orlebar laughed. '*Famulus minimus*, then! You

27

shall offer the least required. . . Now I'll stop teasing, and you'll get off home, young Welfare. Lewis is no lord, though for sure his blood's better than mine. Now do you remember firm and clear, Thomas – my young kinsman need a friend. He's naun now but me – and my sister, God save her – to cosset and care for him.' His voice roughening into country accents made Thomas feel more at home. Such words as *famulus* and *Phoebus* had left him floundering. 'Never look so straight, boy. Friendship stands n'forcing. So – let be howt'will.'

Thomas went home with his head whirling. He took the place of the delivered sacks on the donkey's back and proceeded at the animal's own pace. Boys love a mystery, Master Orlebar had said. . . But not all mysteries are solved, and Thomas knew already in his heart that he might never know even if Lewis Mallory had brothers or sisters, or if his mother, too, had been ready to banish him. Perhaps silence was friendship at its best, a trusting acceptance of tales that would never be told. Companionship would be willingly paid for in this fashion – yet Thomas knew how he would need to tell a friend about Betsy, about his plans for going after her, of his need to be helped on the way. The donkey's uneasy trot shook up Thomas's thoughts and he felt as wise as an abbot. If he was to give friendship and Lewis was to take it, Thomas thought at this moment that he could be content. The matter seemed to slip down deep into his conscience. He would not speak of it to Agnes, except to say the boy was there at Ghylls Hatch.

They were jogging past the hidden milepost when Thomas saw a black horse approaching down the track, a woman in the saddle. Thomas knew her at once – Dame Elizabeth FitzEdmund, a widow of fortune, living at the big house that stood eastward of Ghylls Hatch, that was called Mantlemass. The lady had not lived long in these parts. At first she had startled the neighbourhood by her forthright manner, so little like anyone's idea of such a woman. But her worth had soon been recognized. She was now spoken of with respect. She employed a big household and had recently engaged in the breeding of coney for the use of their pelts. It was a triumph for a newcomer to be so speedily accepted by foresters, who disliked and suspected any stranger unless he might be a fugitive from justice. Even the young stranger at Ghylls Hatch would need to prove himself.

Dame Elizabeth called out as soon as she saw Thomas. He slipped off the donkey's back and ran on his own much faster feet, for such a call from such a lady was a summons indeed.

'My horse has a shoe needs a farrier's attention,' she said in her strong fine voice. 'Have you been at Ghylls Hatch, child? Did you note if their smithy's firing?'

'Yes, madam. And No,' said Thomas, to pay her out for calling him *child*.

'What does that mean?'

'Yes, madam, I were to Ghylls Hatch; No, madam, I never did note the smithy, hot or cold.'

'Well, then, my pert young master,' she said, sharpish, 'what did you note?'

Thomas's more obvious news came tumbling out of him like oats from a sack.

'Master Orlebar's mare, Dido, give birth this very day. The foal shall be named Roman. Master Orlebar say I should choose, and so I said Roman. There was another there said it should be Phoebus. But Master Orlebar, he took my name, Roman. The other I tell of is Master Orlebar's kinsman, new come to the forest. Master Lewis Mallory. His cousin. He look mighty swarly come Master Orlebar speak of *Roman* for the foal!'

'I know of him,' she said. 'So his father sent him to be a country lad.'

'Aye, madam – and he's looking none so sprackish, neither.'

She flicked up her strongly-marked eyebrows. '*Sprackish?* What's *sprackish?*'

'It mean perked-up, surelye,' he said, amazed that so well-set-up a soul should seem so ignorant. 'Only perked-up he were not.' He was bothered to see that the lady was only just not laughing at him. 'Well then, madam – he do look most particular. Jawled-out,' he added hopefully.

'You mean he looked sick – unhappy?'

Thomas only nodded, not wanting to put the matter into further words.

'I'll not have young creatures unhappy in my

neighbourhood,' Dame Elizabeth said, frowning now. 'What's your name?'

'Thomas, madam, Thomas Welfare.'

'The miller's boy? Tell the miller, then, my people are bringing him the end of last year's grain. It's good. It'll pay for good milling. After – we must wait for the new crop.' She nodded to him and moved on her way, saying she would seek out the Ghylls Hatch smith for help. 'Good-day to you, Thomas Welfare.'

'Good-day, lady,' he said, tugging at his forelock respectfully.

He watched her round the curve in the track, then rushed for home. Coming up the last slow incline, speeding on the donkey by running alongside and slapping him encouragingly on the rump, he saw the mill sails still against the hot wide sky. Then he saw the clothes Agnes had hung on the line, and then he saw Agnes herself, her arms upstretched as she pegged out the last garment, her own petticoat she was so proud of, that Betsy had stitched and sent her last Christmastide by the pedlar. There in the hot sunshine, unstirred by any breath of breeze, hung Gaffer's best shirt and his miller's cap and apron, and Thomas's only good hose, worn some Sundays but seldom any other time. There, too, carefully smoothed after wringing, hung the bed-healing their grandmother had woven of snippets when she was a girl, and brought with her when she came here as the miller's bride – fifty years later, when she lay dying, it was still her covering. All the rest of the long line was taken up with flour sacks, washed and bleached, as only Agnes knew how.

'Summat to tell thee, Agnes Welfare,' Thomas shouted, slapping the donkey off to graze, then running to his sister.

'And summat to tell *thee*,' she answered, rushing straight into the matter before he could open his mouth. 'Miles was here. Did any tell you Dan Morphew's moved to live atop Clinkerbank? Got himself a hovel there, Miles tell, and building better. But it's not a house he's come to building now.'

'A castle?' Thomas asked, puzzled. 'A church?'

'A mill,' said Agnes.

3. News of Betsy

'Keep it from Gaffer, long as we may,' Agnes decided. 'The thatch'll fair fly from the rafters, come he get to hear.'

'If Miles tell of it, then it's all about.'

'Keep mum, I tell you. Let it rest.'

Thomas looked at Agnes and then away. He saw she was flustered – *vlothered* was the word he would have used – and he knew very well why. If the new mill were bigger, better, faster – as it might well be, set on that fine height where the trees had been cleared – then Gospels Mill had as well close down. That would be well for Agnes, for their grandfather would be obliged to resign himself to sitting quiet for the rest of his days – and where else but in the home that Agnes and Miles would make together. As for Thomas, he would be free to find his own way. Miles was a woodman and carpenter. If Thomas settled to work for him – and Miles would certainly be happy for him to do so – then he would never see the world, never get back to Betsy. He would not work for Miles, one way or another he would leave the forest – and yet the thought that he might be nearer to it than ever before excited him less than it might have done even yesterday.

'There's never need for two mills set so close, Agnes. Gospels must fall on evil times. Dan Morphew's no ancient man like our Gaffer.'

'Never talk so rafty, brother! Dan Morphew's an upstart. Though he'm cousin to the Reeve. Our own grandfather's father were first miller hereabouts.' She was flushed and almost shrill. She wore her dark hair screwed back from her healthy face, so there was no hiding -her feelings. 'Give over gawping!' she cried. 'And hold your tongue come I tell you.'

Thomas had never known before how much Agnes longed to get settled as Miles Hoad's wife, how staunchly she stood by her promise to their father to care for Gaffer till the end of his working days. . .

A week later, the still summer weather was cooled by a fine breeze blowing over the downs from the sea. Great clouds, dazzling white, rushed and tumbled over the bright sky. The mill was luffed into the wind, swung on its pivoting mainpost, its four great sweeps tearing round, the wind screaming against the cloth taut along the wooden sail spars. Inside, chains rattled, wheels meshed, the great stones ground like the gnashing molars of a king of giants. The entire structure shook and rattled, groaned and roared and fought with the wind. The grain gushed from the bin and into the spout that led it by way of the hopper to be fed to the whirring stones. Below was Thomas, seeing to the sacks, tugging on the chain hoist to signal as each one filled. It all ran to a rhythm old and familiar, but no miller or miller's

35

boy could afford to forget the dangers of the rumbling monster's insides that could tear at limb or scalp. When Thomas was first set to work for his grandfather he had been eight years old and terrified. Even now, though he had the measure of the place, he treated it with the respect it deserved. 'Sacks to fill and men to kill, Men to kill and sacks to fill, And both to tumble down the hill,' was a familiar chant of his grandfather's.

But in this fair spell of perfect working weather, all was cheerful. Old Welfare was full of plans he'd been promising for years to put into action.

'Power'n plenty to drive a second pair o' stones,' he shouted over the noise of the mill at work. 'Did I tell ever of a mill I once hear spoke of – had eight sweeps?'

'You did so, gaffer,' Thomas yelled back. 'A hundred times over,' he added to himself.

'Then I tell agin, and keep it in thy scaddle young head – it's what'll turn at Gospels yet!'

'Turn it over, more like.'

'What's that?'

'Naun,' said Thomas, grinning.

In mid afternoon of a hard working day, Thomas, waiting for a sack to fill, saw Agnes peering into the body of the mill and signalling wildly, though she could not make herself heard. The sack was all but ready. Thomas waited a second or two more, then jerked at the hoist. The mill quietened a fraction as his grandfather, on the floor above, braked gingerly.

'Pedlar's coming!' yelled Agnes. 'Tell Gaffer!'

She was gone instantly. Thomas looked up and saw the old man's feet on the floor above, as he tended wheels and stones and grain feed. His skilled care with the brake impressed Thomas as always. The hole above him suddenly filled with his grandfather's face, his beard and eyebrows full of chaff, his cap tight down on his forehead, his eyes sharp and glaring.

'What come to you, down there?'

'It's the higgler, gaffer. Old Turnberry come. Agnes said to tell you.'

'Better things to do than go nabbling wi' any higgler.'

'Packthread!' Thomas bellowed, his voice cracking. 'We need packthread!'

'Goo on and buy, then, ye lazy lad – and see that sack's set upright. *Wait!* Yon line's kinking.'

By the time Thomas had settled everything to his grandfather's satisfaction the pedlar, Jonas Turnberry, had reached the Welfares' plat and was hailing Agnes. He drove a small cart, pulled by a rough brown pony, old and half blind. They travelled the countryside at their own pace, and trade was always brisk. Jonas carried a large and varied stock – wooden things like stirring spoons and milking stools and cunningly carved boxes; soft goods such as threads and ribbons and bolts of cloth, laces and thonging; also sometimes spices from distant parts of the world, come by at markets and fairs, held in towns or villages near the coast, or at actual ports. He carried toys, too – carved animals, dolls with

37

wooden painted faces, rattles for infants, made of ozier, sometimes with a tiny bell inside instead of just beans or seeds. He had awls, nails and needles, crocks of tallow for candle-making, bladders of lard. At apple time he brought big red-cheeked fruit to the forest, where the only apples were small and green and wild, taking away honey for those who lived bee-less in towns.

But best of all, Jonas Turnberry carried news, gossip, messages, gifts from one member of a family to another far away – and today he brought a packed basket from Betsy, at whose door, so long a journey from the forest, he called twice in the year.

'She say to keep it upstanding, and so I done,' Jonas told Agnes.

'Oh what can it be?' cried Agnes. 'Come quick, Thomas – there's word from Betsy. And is she well, Jonas? Her time come any day, as I reckon from your last call wi' news of her.'

'It come ten days gone when I saw her, and that were May, early on.'

'Oh there, oh there!' cried Agnes in such great delight that she instantly broke into tears. 'And is all well? Oh I prayed hard to have her well delivered. . . Boy or girl, higgler?'

'Boy. Wi' black hair, a nose, two eyes like peri-winkles, and all the usual number of arms, legs and other parts.' The pedlar was beaming all over his big face, for though he most of all delighted in a tale of disaster, good news was nearly as enjoyable. 'And if her brother were

39

but nigh enough,' he said, 'he'd have a godson to his name. So I was to tell thee, Thomas Welfare.'

'Shall she call the babe Thomas, then?' He felt half shy at the thought, yet warmed right through by the message of affection Betsy had thus sent him. 'I'll never get to seeing the brat,' he grumbled. 'Plague on it.'

Agnes gave a cry and slapped out at him. 'Take that word off'n your wicked tongue! And pray God you never pay for it!' She shuddered and crossed herself. 'Bad enough our gaffer speak loose, brother Thomas. If you must come to swearing – choose otherly!'

'Open the basket,' Jonas Turnberry said. 'Open and see what Goody Betsy sent or you'll be the daysend quarrelling.'

Agnes whipped off the cloth that covered the basket. Inside was a great cask, cool in a rush-plaited cover. Agnes would have tugged out the bung to sniff at the contents, only Jonas stopped her.

'Never spoil it, woman! Wait on drinking time. Elder-flower wine – and she took great trouble to have it clear and sparkling. . . See what else she send you.'

There was a round, dark cake, stuffed with raisins, a cheese of goat's milk, a crock of butter strongly salted to preserve it, but already proclaiming how long the pedlar had been on his way. There was also a pair of plaited rag slippers, which were what Miller Welfare liked best of all to wear on tired feet – if ever he got to sitting easy by the fire, which was not often.

'Tell my sister how sore we still miss her company,'

said Agnes, wiping her eyes, 'and her dear clever skills about the house. . . And now, pedlar, what we need from you is packthread and needles. Also a good birchbroom and long nails – if you thought get such at the forge.'

'I've the nails. I know for certain what my customers will need. . . But there's still a thing in the basket. For you, young Thomas. A nativity gift. Soon moving to your twelfth year, your sister say you should remember.'

'I do remember! Quick, Agnes – what gift's she send?'

Agnes had barely forgiven him for using the word *plague*. What she took from the basket she handed to him almost reluctantly, as if he deserved nothing and should by rights get nothing. But he grinned at her and snatched, and she held on, beginning to laugh, hiding the package behind her back – then tossing it to him so that he barely caught it.

'Show, then,' said Jonas Turnberry.

It was a round red cap of felted cloth, bright and warm. Thomas turned it in his hands, grinning with pleasure. Then he clapped it on his head and began strutting up and down like any scarlet-crowned rooster.

'I never had such before!' he cried.

His strutting turned to capering. He snatched the cap off and tossed it in the air, then caught and spun it and clapped it on again. And like a magic cap it seemed to make him grow. Surely he was taller, broader, his feet bigger, his arms stronger, his voice a man's voice rather than a boy's. . .?

'Your sister say – "Tell'm 'tis his'n to keep or give away." '

'Give away? Never! Never!'

At this moment the miller, his sails set to work on alone, came clattering down the steps and across the goose-cropped grass towards them.

'Did you bring the long nails, higgler? I need 'em sore.' Then he spotted Thomas and cried out, 'That make fine feathers! Better you stick to a miller's white cap, grandson.'

'Our Betsy did send it! It's mine for ever!'

Jonas was counting out the enormous nails, specially forged for such as millers and millwrights.

'Give'm my daughter, then.' He jerked his head at the mill. 'Best not leave her turn alone. Wind's freakish.'

'Aye, best not,' agreed Jonas, now in position for his other piece of news. 'Best turn her while you may, Gaffer Welfare. There's others set to milling in these parts.'

Agnes looked sharply at Jonas, opened her mouth closed it hard. Thomas was still.

'Naun other mill than Gospels,' the old man said.

'Not this day nor tomorrer, maybe. But soon enough.'

Now the old man had paused, though he did not turn back. 'Aye?'

'Aye, surelye. Dan Morphew's setting up on Clinker-bank.'

The miller stood as still as his own four sails on a wind-less day. From under their bushy white eyebrows his sharp, small eyes bored out like stars on a frosty night. Agnes and Thomas, expecting some mighty explosion, could neither of them find any word to prevent it, while Jonas, enjoying the effect he had made, went on to improve his tale.

'Since the reeve ordered'm cut down the beeches, Clinkerbank's a suent catcher of fine winds, miller. New mills run faster'n old, I'd say. And now the lady of Mantlemass got settled wi' a big household, there's a plenty milling to be done.' He shook his head and sighed. 'Hard for Welfare's if trade's to go elsewhere.'

'Let be,' said Agnes. 'Don't heed Jonas, grandfather. His tongue did ever run away wi' him.'

The old man began slowly to curse. Terrible words gushed out as if they had been waiting years to be used to a good purpose. He stood very still and gradually his voice mounted from a rumble to a shout, then to a roar and so to something near a scream. Then the flood died out. Without any further word to those listening, he turned and went back to the mill. He went steadily and briskly, and perhaps only Agnes knew how his hand trembled and his muscles sagged, as he clutched at the rail to haul himself up the wooden steps.

'Oh shame to you!' she cried, thrusting Jonas out of the way and hurrying after her grandfather. 'A sad way to treat an old man!'

The pedlar and Thomas watched her as she went after Welfare into the mill. But he had clearly little time for her. The sails speeded up the moment he was inside,

44

and within seconds Agnes had come out again, her face very red, and called to Thomas to get back to work.

'Seemed fair to give warning,' Jonas excused himself, for Thomas, too, looked black. 'Nothing but flurry about the forest today. There's Ghylls Hatch in a tumble, too.'

'Why there?'

'It seem Master Orlebar have some young kinsman staying – that's quite a gentleman and more, one of the men tell me.'

'Well? Yes? What's the flurry?'

'The lad's took himself off. Left of his own will. And all running to-and-agen to find'm.'

'Left?' said Thomas. 'Left Ghylls Hatch?'

'You might say run away,' Jonas Turnberry replied.

The miller bellowed 'Thomas!' from the doorway. His energy had returned, it seemed.

'Say no word of it to my sister,' Thomas said, quick and urgent.

Then he ran to the mill.

4. Boy on the Run

The forest was both long and wide. It sprawled over great distances. Somewhere in all that expanse of tree and scrub and heathland, one boy was hiding. 'Where'd I go, come I needed?' Thomas asked himself. He knew at once where he would go – but Lewis Mallory had been so short a time in these parts he could not have learnt his way about. There would be many threats to his safety – bogs to catch him by the feet, old minepits deeply flooded where he might stumble and drown, adders that could poison. . . At his first chance, Thomas was running truant from the mill and beating through the forest in search of the runaway. He was no sooner safely out of sight of home than he put up a fine cock pheasant, and five minutes or so after he sent a string of seven young fallow deer bounding – both omens for successful hunting, he decided.

There were others on the same errand as Thomas. As he crouched in the brakes he saw Master Orlebar himself riding. He went by fast, looking stern and anxious. Perhaps Thomas should have called out to him, to let him know he too was about the job – but he preferred to be secret. It gave him a feeling of importance, of deep excitement. He would find Lewis, persuade him home, be praised and thanked by Master Orlebar. His grandfather would be filled with astonished respect, Agnes with love and admiration. It was a comfortable picture.

The way he took had hazards of its own, but they were well known. He slid down steep banks, hurled himself across small chasms, walked along stream beds where there was no other way. Often he was following deer tracks that tunnelled through dense scrub, among trees sick and suffering from having their bark stripped by the deer. Many small animals, disturbed by his passing, scuttled stealthily away; wood pigeons clattered. He came out from a tangled stretch of country to wade across a small river. It ran fast, tinkling over boulders with deep pools between, the water stained red where it surged over iron stone. He was in mid-stream when someone called to him and he froze, standing on one leg in the water like a heron.

'Wait, young Thomas – wait for me!' The man who hailed him was Peter Crutten, one of the men from Ghylls Hatch – a cousin of Miles Hoad. 'Wait, now, do!' Peter cried, and he came scrambling down the bank, hanging on to his horse's bridle. The horse dug in halfway down, straining back on its haunches, so Peter was bound to stop.

'What, then?' cried Thomas, swarly as any old badger cornered and set upon. 'What d'you want? I'm busy.'

'Did you see a sign o' young Master Lewis Mallory,

47

my master's young kinsman? Did you see'm or any place he might be hid, as you come by?'

'I see Master Orlebar ride by.'

'Ah, poor soul – he's sore frit summat bad befall. The young gentleman run off two days gone.'

'I never saw'm.'

'Well – best he go hungry. He'll be druv home soon enough – so being no evil fall to him.'

'I'll have an eye open.'

'You do, Thomas. His cousin's a fine gift for'm when he come home safe to Ghylls Hatch.'

If Thomas so plagued his family he knew well there'd be a beating at homecoming, not a gift. No doubt Master Orlebar thought to lure a wandering dog by trailing a juicy bone. Very slightly, Thomas's feelings inclined away from the fugitive.

'What gift? So I'll tell him.'

'There's a prime young horse waiting to be called his'n.'

The swift water was now very chill over Thomas's feet. He scrambled to the far bank, but there was such black envy in his heart he all but gave up and turned for home. It seemed bitter indeed that what he needed so badly should be offered as a bribe to the gentleman's son. He went fast up the steep slope from the water, and as he came over the brow, he saw before him that wilderness which few would have chosen to enter, but which he had made his own. The lure of the place was too much for him, and he pressed forward, wading

48

waist-high through bracken that at his last visit had
barely unfurled. He had marked his path long ago with
knife cuts on sapling birches, and he made his way swift
and easy, thrusting back brambles that had thrown out
new wandering shoots, treading down many small white
starry flowers, growing thickly about the roots of the
trees – in spring, primroses possessed this ground.

It was very quiet. Filtering through the fine branches

and small leaves of the birch, the sun was unusually yellow. There were many strange and beautiful mosses on old stumps, on humps of stone. This was the most secret spot in Thomas's world. It was here he would hide, if ever he were on the run – but it would need a very resourceful guardian angel to bring Lewis Mallory to such a hidden place.

Ahead of him the ground fell away gently, then dropped into speedily increasing darkness. Beyond again, a high bank rose and blocked the way completely, humping to an overhang of bramble and briar, all roped up with honeysuckle vines. There was a shallow bowl made by a spring dropping from the overhang and disappearing into a spread of bright mossy ground. But most important was the cave that ran back magically into deep darkness, then turned into a warm dry chamber with light filtering from some undiscovered shaft. When he was most at odds with his grandfather, most lonely for Betsy, Thomas would think of running here, living on coney and squirrel and gamebirds cooked over a fire of birch twigs and pine kernels, on berries and crab apples and what he called 'misheroons'.

As he came to the place now, he planted himself foursquare before the mouth of the cave, and called out –

'Come you forth, Lewis Mallory!'

His voice astonished him. He had not heard it for far more than an hour, and it cracked sadly instead of ringing out bold and commanding.

There was an echo here that he had never heard before, since he had always stayed quiet in the place. It made him jump and spring back, as if to be out of reach of a monster. A pair of startled jays set up a wild screeching, and so disturbed other birds, which flashed and flicked and chattered about the trees, the small ones setting the leaves fluttering, the larger leaving swaying branches behind them as they fled.

No human sound answered Thomas's cry – but as he stood waiting for the stillness to settle again, a trickle of sand and small stones fell from the high bank ahead, as if a foot had shifted on the brink.

Alarmed, Thomas sprang back even further, so that a tree trunk was between him and whatever lurked. He looked up cautiously through the tangle. From the rim of the mound, Lewis Mallory was staring down at him.

'Wait!' cried Thomas, dashing forward, wild with triumph and excitement, starting the echo again. 'Wait! Wait, I tell you!'

Wait! called the echo, back and back.

The other boy, however, gave little sign of being likely to run. He stood staring down, and now Thomas was as still as if he watched some rare creature which, once let go, might never in life be seen again. Then Lewis moved at last. He began to pick his way down to Thomas, scrambling and sliding on his bottom until he reached firm ground.

'You find it, then,' said Thomas; and somehow he sounded proud of Lewis for being so resourceful.

There was a kind of frail dignity about the fugitive
that was increased by comparison with Thomas's stocky
country build and sun-browned face. The boy was dirty,
bloody where he had been torn by brambles and undergrowth; he looked hungry.

'Find it. . .? Found it? Found what?'

'The cave. The cave for hiding. They told how
you come to run away. I hoped you should find the
cave.'

'I saw you from the track across the valley. I followed

you down. If you think to go unseen – then leave that red cap at home.'

Lewis sounded both fierce and despairing, as any boy might after two long days and nights wandering in strange territory, and with an increasingly empty belly.

'I brought you a snoule o' bread,' said Thomas, holding out the heel of a loaf brought from home, rather as he might hold out an apple to a reluctant pony. It was truly pitiful to see how the other boy snatched the bread, gnawing at it, munching without any word, until every crumb was gone. Then he scooped his hands under the spring and drank, and wiped his wet mouth with the back of his hand. Then at last he eyed Thomas as Thomas was eyeing him.

'You must bring me some more. And before night.'

'Nay, not then!' cried Thomas, uneasy at this commanding approach. 'There's naun enough at home to give away twice in one day.' He looked at Lewis who had folded his arms across himself, as if he had to hug his hunger to keep it from bursting out. 'Best you get along home,' said Thomas, quiet as any timmersome girl.

'Home? Where's home?'

'Ghylls Hatch, surelye.'

'Say, "Go to your new home". I'll never see my true home any more.'

'What come to you, then?' asked Thomas, not meaning to ask, because of certain thoughts he had laboured with after their first meeting.

'That I'll never tell!' cried Lewis, pale and fierce. 'Never. Never to you or any man. How should I? It's already forgotten.'

'Shan't you go tell Master Orlebar you'm safe? He's sorely set-about.'

'I shall go to sea. You're to help me. A cabin boy. It's a terrible life, they say. How far's the sea?'

'There and back's a day's ride. All but. I never saw it.'

'Come too. That means only one journey and no going back.' He looked sharply at Thomas. 'You're grinning. What did I say to make you jeer?'

'I did smile only. You speak s'fast and strange.'

Lewis looked at him, or so Thomas thought, as if he saw him fair and square for the first time. There flashed across his face something of that look they had shared at Ghylls Hatch, when they laughed together at schoolmasterly Roger Orlebar. 'Shall you be a friend to me, Thomas Welfare?'

'I'm the miller's boy,' said Thomas, hot with pleasure that his name was remembered.

'What of it? That means two of us against all the grizzlebeards. Still – if I'm too good for you. . .'

'That's for you to say,' said Thomas, beginning to feel pestered, yet strangely longing to save the vanity of the poor fugitive – for all his bluster he did often sound near to tears.

'It's for *you!*'

'For both, then. Both say, Aye.'

'Very well. Then we must swear loyalty, each to each. Have you a knife? I lost mine on the way.'

Feeling very much as if nothing in life was to be simple any more, Thomas tugged out his knife and handed it to Lewis.

'This is a thing both knights and savages think fit,' said Lewis. He set his teeth, drew the blade sharp across the ball of his thumb and ordered Thomas to do the same. Thomas found it painful, the line of bright red beads springing along the separated skin made him feel squeamish. 'Now place your hand on mine,' Lewis ordered. 'This is the blood of true friends mingling.'

'What shall that do for us?' asked Thomas.

'Such friends become brothers.'

If Thomas had been wrestling with a nervous desire to grin at this solemn magic, the word *brother* banished the impulse.

'So swear to be my brother in all things,' Lewis said. 'And I shall do the same. No, wait! It has to be a true oath, and a solemn.'

He pulled at a leather thong he was wearing round his neck under his shirt. There was a ring attached, big, golden, with some design on its face. This should be the talisman, he said, on which they would swear allegiance.

'It is my father's ring. I stole it. I've nothing else of what I used to be. Now, Thomas – put your hand over mine as I hold this ring and swear the oath as I tell it you.' He thought a moment, and then said, *'By this ring and by this hand and by the blood shed between us to signify true friendship, I swear to be Lewis Mallory's brother in all things, as so he swears to be mine.'*

Thomas repeated the words, stumbling over them, for they were too grand for his countryman's round voice. Once Lewis gave a quick snort of laughter, when Thomas got muddled, but there was no unkindness in it – he was looking at Thomas now as if he were a person newly made and important. Then he took the oath in his turn. Each boy crossed himself to make the thing noted down in heaven, and Lewis then shoved the ring back into hiding. He licked the blood off his cut thumb and winced a bit.

'It bleeds a good deal. How's yours?'

'Mortacious tender,' said Thomas. 'Wait'll I find us some gossamer.'

He ran into the cave and scooped at the cobwebs that hung above dry shelves and crannies in the rock. The blood dried when he had clapped the stuff on both wounds. The drama was then over for the time being – but their problems remained.

'I'm bitter hungry,' Lewis said.

'Get you on home, then, friend. Let you end your cousin's frenzy and froudening. You'd seem then great and noble.' *Noble* was a word Thomas had never until now had occasion to use. It sounded both strange and fine to him. He repeated it, like some rule just learnt. 'Noble,' he said. 'Surelye.' But Lewis said nothing in reply.

The afternoon was wearing away fast and by now

Thomas, too, would be missed. Old as he was, his grandfather's beating arm could still contrive a powerful stroke. The strange word Master Orlebar had used slipped back into Thomas's mind – *fam* something. It meant among other more pleasant things, whipping-boy. The recollection gave Thomas one more inkling of what friendship might mean. If he stayed on here he would get his beating, but until he could persuade Lewis back to Ghylls Hatch he would not return home; he must take the punishment, as if for both of them.

He was concerned for Lewis's wan and filthy appearance – he looked a proper fluttergrub. What Peter Crutten had spoken of became now a bargaining point, rather than a matter for stupid jealousy.

'I hear your cousin have a fine gift for you. It were Peter Crutten tell me.'

'What gift?'

'A riding horse,' said Thomas, watching Lewis's face that seemed full of contradictions.

'What's that to me? I've had plenty.' Then after a second or two's silence he said, 'It might be Solitaire. . .'

Thomas saw the idea working its way through Lewis's mind and his anxiety was great. If this temptation failed, he would not know what else to offer.

'He is a very kindly man,' said Lewis at last, half to himself.

'And you did make him a fearful one,' Thomas told him, beginning to pray hard and silently for some assistance. The prayer was surely heard.

'Come with me, then,' Lewis said.

'As far as I may. I've work to do.'

'Then set me on my way. . .'

All through the heavy tangle and along the deer path the two went silently. They crossed the river together, and when they were on the far side of the ghyll Lewis looked about him and said he could remember the rest.

The light was now going fast, the sun had vanished and a dull sky promised rain before nightfall. Thomas let Lewis go but followed him silent and unseen on a parallel path, watching that he did not lose his way. And at a spot where the track divided, Lewis did pause and look round and seem to smell the air doubtfully Now that he was alone his hunger and weariness, and the heaviness of defeat, were on him like a sack on a miller's back. He sat down under a tree and leant back wearily against the trunk, then slumped forward and laid his head on his knees. Thomas would have come out of hiding to help him, but decency held him back – he feared that Lewis was quietly crying.

A woman on a black horse was riding briskly along the track below where Thomas crouched in hiding. He recognized Dame Elizabeth FitzEdmund, and she must have seen Lewis from some way back, for she now checked her horse and came on slowly. A few paces from the boy she halted and called his name, too softly for Thomas to hear. Lewis, who might have leapt up and ran, stayed where he was – though he got to his feet and muttered some greeting. Not scorning to eavesdrop, Thomas shifted a good deal nearer.

At first, Dame Elizabeth spoke to Lewis from the saddle, but then she dismounted, and with the bridle over her arm went to stand by him.

'Are you lost? And if you are – such tears from a lad of your years!'

'I ran from Ghylls Hatch, two days past,' he said.

'Aye – well I know it. And that good man half out of his wits on your account. Get home – get home. Never stay skulking like a snivelling coward.'

'I'm hungry,' Thomas heard Lewis say.

She laughed at that, telling him he knew well enough where he should find food.

'Come, then – rouse up and get on your way. And do you consider, Lewis Mallory, that there are not so many of my own sort hereabouts that I'll scorn you for a neighbour... Now tell me you'll have sense enough not to run away again.'

He nodded that he had sense, and shook his head about running away again. Thomas's heart lifted. He saw Lewis run off along the path ahead. Dame Elizabeth stood watching him for some time, before she remounted and rode on her way. And Thomas stayed watching both, till both were out of sight and he could turn for home.

Agnes was already out looking for him. He saw her

before she saw him, for the bracken on the home track had grown taller than he was and even his red cap was hidden. When at last she saw him, Agnes waved her arms wildly, looking rather like a small windmill standing ahead of the big one.

'Gaffer looked for you!' she cried, as Thomas came near. 'The wind sprang till the sun went and he got to milling. None else but me to take your place. You know that pester me cruelly. My hair's full o' chaff and I'm set to sneezing my head silly!'

'Where's he to, then?' Thomas asked, not really wanting to know.

'In the barn, now. Locked in there. It's one of his mad days, I'd say.'

Thomas did not like the sound of it. He crossed the plat reluctantly and sidled along to the barn door. He set his eye against one of the cracks and peered in. He saw at once what Agnes had meant; the old man looked very wild. The inside of the enormous barn was lit by no fewer than seven rough torches, stuck into cressets and flaring alarmingly among so much wood. Thomas knew how to get into the barn even though the big doors were barred. The ground was scooped out in a hollow beneath them and he lay down and rolled under.

'Come here, boy,' the miller said at once, though he had not so much as glanced over his shoulder. 'Come here, I say, Thomas.'

Ordinarily he would by now have reached out for a stick – but there was something else afoot.

'Come here, you – come close!' the old man cried, almost dancing with impatience. 'Look well where I tell thee. What's to see?'

He had been drawing with a stick on the earthen floor of the barn, scratching a great design that reached from side to side. Thomas's heart dropped at the sight, down where his boots could have caught it, had he been wearing any. 'It's the six-sailer, gaffer.' To carry that number Gospels would need to be half as high again, but more than twice as sturdy, and solid as a castle tower. She already swayed to her own four sweeps.

'Only this day, boy, I see how to rig her. First-time-ever, I see it! Let Dan Morphew set up better!'

'But this is Gospels Mill, gaffer,' Thomas said quickly. 'There's four sweeps wi' four names. Come there's six to trim – there's no names for'm.'

Old Welfare laughed. He began to walk the length and breadth of his design, sometimes hopping like a goblin from one point to the next, as if already the solid sails lay waiting to be hauled aloft and he must take care not to step on them or fall over them. And as he went in this eerie fashion about the torchlit barn he chanted:

> 'One for Matthew, one for Mark –
>   One for Lucifer, seen in the dark.
> One for Luke and one for John –
>   One for Beelzebub, Satan's son!'

It was the most dreadful jingle of the many he had

made. Thomas chilled and shivered to hear it. Bad enough to imagine six sails turning on a body six times too frail. But to call two of them after fiends out of hell was also blasphemy. It might well call down fire and brimstone on them all.

5. Two Boys . . .

There came a spell of bright weather, fine-winded, with blue sky and bowling white clouds. Thomas and his grandfather were working every hour of every day, for any man within miles who had grain for grinding seized on the time to send his sacks to Gospels Mill. On the floor of the big barn the scratched pattern of a six-sailed mill gradually became scuffed and lost under the passage of many feet. Neither Thomas nor his grandfather spoke again of the two new sails and their terrible names. For all that, when the mill was roaring and clattering, shaking and swishing, the old man could still be heard singing to himself – and Thomas, though he was unable to distinguish words or tune, knew all the same what song he sang.

After three long weeks the wind dropped, the sun withdrew. The blue sky was veiled, a drizzling rain fell all day till evening, when it cleared to a still and steamy silence. Old Welfare, as always at such times, then pulled off his miller's cap, pulled on one more ancient, his nightcap, and took himself to bed. He would sleep for three days if the weather stayed windless, waking only to eat and drink, and that but once in the day. Thomas and Agnes had the place to themselves, Miles came to supper each evening, and then he and Agnes sat on the bench that stood against the cottage wall, holding hands, enjoying the quiet, looking out over the forest steaming after the day's rain and saying very little; sometimes one or the other turned and smiled.

On the evening of the third quiet day, the sun came out but the air stayed still. Thomas stood sharpening his knife on the big stone by the well-head and remembering the brotherhood oath, of which the only outward sign was the fast healing scar along his thumb. In all this time he had neither seen nor heard from Lewis Mallory and the whole matter was beginning to seem a dream. He was taking great care with the knife, which had a finely tempered blade, when he became aware of a rider approaching up the track. He did not look up, but whistled, pulled a hair from his head and tested the knife cautiously. Then someone shouted and he was bound to look up, hearing his own name.

'Thomas! Thomas Welfare! Come here! Come quickly!'

Thomas then went slowly forward to the head of the track. He saw Lewis Mallory bareback on a satiny chestnut. Half reluctant, half eager, scowling rather than smiling, Thomas sauntered down the track and stood short of the bank from which Lewis had hailed him. As Lewis came level he slid off the horse's back and holding him as much by the mane as the bridle cried to Thomas – 'Here, quick! Take a turn with him! See how sweet he treads! A pace like silk, he has – see for yourself. Here – come on! I'll give you a leg up.'

Still without speaking, Thomas allowed himself to be set up on the creature's elegant back.

'It *is* Solitaire,' Lewis said. 'Remember when you told me he was waiting at home? I said it could be – and so it is. . . I'll lead a bit till he's used to you.'

'Truly your'n – is he?'

'All but mine. I must learn to be his groom before I set my name to him – so my cousin Orlebar says. I never learnt anything of such work till now. Old Awcock's making me a saddle – and I must know how to tend leather, too, it seems.'

The change in Lewis was amazing. His air of frailty was quite gone. He looked, Thomas decided, as if he had been fed all these weeks on the fat of the land and only now released to show himself to the world. Good health shone in him and his sun-tanned skin matched Thomas's. Now it was possible to see that, however wide apart in birth, they were both boys of flesh and blood, bone and hair. Besides all this, the look of dull misery was gone from Lewis's face, his eyes were clear. Whatever it was that his past held, that Thomas knew he must never expect to learn, Lewis had found a way to set his back to it and his face to the future. It would be the wisdom and kindness of Master Orlebar, Thomas knew, that had brought about the change.

'Now walk him on,' Lewis ordered.

Solitaire tossed his head, moved forward, gathered

65

into speed, reached the top of the track in good order – and stopped dead with all four feet at the sight of the windmill.

'Hang on!' shouted Lewis.

It was doomed advice. Thomas went sailing off into the bracken. He managed to hang on to the bridle, and was dragged like a ship's anchor through the waves of rain-soaked greenery until Lewis reached him and checked the horse. No damage was done, except to Thomas's pride.

'I never rid naun but a donkey till this day,' he admitted, struggling to his feet and rubbing his seat, but grinning all the same.

'I should have asked,' said Lewis. 'You're not hurt, brother?'

The sting was taken out of the business. 'Bum's bruised, reckon, brother,' Thomas answered him.

'It was the mill. I should've thought. Come on and we'll go another way. You must try him again. He's gentle when he knows you. . . Are you sure no harm came to you?' Lewis insisted, peering into Thomas's face. 'He had me off the first time I mounted. I was stiff as wet leather next day.'

'So'll I be, come morrer!'

'Get up again quickly. He must know he's not scared you.'

Thomas gritted his teeth. 'Joss me up, then.' And since Lewis had been so courteous, he added, 'If it do please you.'

This time he felt twice himself. He walked Solitaire on at once, no longer feeling that he was balanced on a knife edge. He held the bridle firmer and felt the young horse resist, toss up his head, then settle. As they moved forward, they moved this time together. Lewis was running alongside – then, as if realizing that the matter now was between horse and rider, he fell back, was left behind. Thomas sat down harder and the rhythm of the horse's easy stride became a part of his own breathing and the beat of his heart. He should have been content with that alone, but he could not resist touching his bare heels to the chestnut's shining flanks. It was indeed only a touch, but Solitaire instantly lengthened his gentle pace to a long canter. The air rushed past Thomas's ears, the hair was combed off his forehead, he opened his mouth as if he would swallow the breeze. Again he used his heel, confident and excited, and again Solitaire changed his stride – this time with a reach forward into a hard gallop. They were off, they were away. Ahead, the forest rose over great stretches of heather and broom. Larks soared as rider and horse swept them from the ground. Thomas sat down harder and harder, his mouth closed now, his teeth clenched, his hands steady.

It seemed as if Solitaire might go for ever. Yet Thomas knew that he held him – and even if that might be through the creature's fine nature rather than his own ability, it was enough. As they breasted a far rise, he saw ahead of him a part of the forest he had rarely visited. He

was level with the ruins of the old palace, that had been a king's hunting lodge. Its chapel, still intact, stood up stark among the broken stone and splintered wood of the rest. In its doorway as he approached, Thomas saw the priest, Sir James; he lived solitary in that place, tending the chapel, saying his office round the clock, celebrating daily mass most often with one of the local farm boys for server and no congregation whatsoever.

The track turned here, scooping away to westward. Thomas began to pull in Solitaire but without response.

Unable to halt him, Thomas at least succeeded in bringing his head round, so that they faced back the way they had come. Then he began to fight the chestnut, whose purpose it had become to unseat his rider. Now the way was downhill and for the first time Thomas's excitement turned in upon itself and threatened to become fear. He knew enough to know he must not saw at the creature's mouth but use wilier ways. He was determined to hang on at any cost, and if he had not been certain that all his hope lay in the bridle, he would have been content with winding his hands in Solitaire's mane. But it was not enough merely to hang on. He had to be master. He crouched over Solitaire's beautiful froth-flecked neck and spoke close by his ear.

Whatever it was he said, and the words must have come to him by instinct out of the long history of man and horse, Solitaire snorted, slowed, shook his head, slowed further, and then, shivering, dropped to a walk.

Thomas would not forget how they paced sedately back and met Lewis toiling up the hill on foot, his face a thunder cloud.

'You fool!' he shouted. 'You could have broken his neck and your own! Jesu, what a lather you've put him in! He's too young for such handling – if harm's come to him my cousin Orlebar shall never forgive me – and I shall never forgive you!'

Thomas slid from Solitaire's back, just managing to find enough strength in his knees to keep himself upright. He watched Lewis run round the horse, feeling him all over, quarter by quarter – and seeming, Thomas thought, half regretful to find nothing wrong, so keen was he to vent his anger.

Thomas said nothing. He was certain he could not have harmed the horse. There had been no slip, no stumble, only that glorious long easy gallop. He waited for Lewis's mood to change, waited for him to say, even grudgingly, 'You did well.' It would come. He was sure of it. He had only to be patient, as any man should be to a friend and brother.

'I'll walk him home,' Lewis said at last. But still he did not so much as glance at Thomas.

'Best I come too, then – lest there's any blame.'

They went on in silence, one behind the other on the narrow way, the horse gradually cooling and quieting. They were in sight of Ghylls Hatch before Lewis paused and turned.

'Come in to my cousin, if you so please. But there'll be no blame. But come all the same.'

'Shall you tell him I did ride?'

'I shall tell him you rode like a knight, Thomas Welfare.'

In spite of their vow of brotherhood, its solemnity, the dramatic business of mingling blood, it was on the day that Thomas rode Lewis's chestnut, Solitaire, that the boys became truly aware of one another. From that time, Thomas never woke to a new day without wondering if their paths might cross, while Lewis took for granted that any enterprise or adventure would be undertaken, if at all possible, in Thomas's company. It was a company Thomas could not always give and he had very often to watch a disgruntled Lewis stalking away down the track. Thomas would dash up to the top floor of the mill to watch Lewis as far as he could – for the pleasure of finding a willing companion after so long on his own quite made up for any immediate disappointment. And as he gazed out between the braked sails Thomas had the further satisfaction of seeing that Lewis would stop now and again – to listen, to peer, to watch – thus proving to Thomas that he was learning about foresty matters.

With the passing on of summertime, Thomas's labour became a little less. The next hard time would be after the harvest. At present most grain from last year was milled and sacked, and many of those sacks empty. The slack time was taken up cleaning and repairing. The sails were let down with the help of Miles Hoad and his father. They were laid on the ground and the miller looked them over inch by inch for flaws, cracks, splintering, tears. It was Agnes's job to inspect and repair the sail cloths, and she was very blithe and cheerful about it, seeing Miles every day and blossoming in consequence. Thomas fetched and carried, steadied ladders, sharpened tools, counted out nails, mixed pitch over a slow fire to caulk leaks and paint the sides of the mill.

Lewis came often to watch, and gradually took his

share of the odd tasks. This shocked Agnes, who could not bear to see him dirty his hands.

'What might Master Orlebar say, come he see such a sight!'

'Agnes, I tell you over and agen – Master Orlebar's set to make him a countryman, You wunna listen! It's fit he should be so – and what foresty lad ever showed clean palms? Or finger nails wi'out they'd black rims from toiling?'

'He's gentle-blooded, Thomas. . .'

'We've a promise. A promise to be brothers.'

She looked so dumbfounded he wished with all his heart he had not spoken. 'Don't tell. . .'

'Tell? I'd never speak such nonsense out loud.'

It was fortunate that Miles arrived to distract her. Better still, he had news to cheer her out of all thoughts of disapproval. In his trade as woodman and carpenter, Miles was much about the forest. He knew it as he might know his father's tenantry acre many, many times multiplied. He knew every track, shaw and spinney, he knew the rivers and how they ran, their waterfalls, all quarries, disused mines, present mines, badger setts, fox holes, coney warrens. He knew where the doe dropped her fawn, where the stags made their stamping grounds in autumn, and how many red and fallow or roe deer might be seen in a day, and all their shiftings from place to place. He could recite the names of the Beasts of the Forest, the Beasts of the Chase, the Beasts and Fowls of the Warren, as they had been set down a hundred years and more ago. Now all this learning was to be rewarded. The Master of the Forest, who held his office these days directly from the crown, had appointed new rangers – and Miles was to be one.

'That mean I'm nearer the building my own dwelling. Nearer to being wed and settling in my own right.'

Agnes had turned bright red with delight.

'When? When shall it be?'

'Spring? Shall you wed me in spring next, Agnes Welfare?'

'But mind not to tell Grandfather yet awhile, Miles. He's stranger than I ever saw these days. His old wits do seem all bent one way – the mill, the mill!'

'Worse to come, then,' Miles said, pulling a long face. 'The mill on Clinkerbank stand out five mile away – right down to Staglye village. Sweeps'll be set by harvest, I'd say. Does he know of it – he never speak of it to me.'

'He knows. But thinks to beat all yet – i'n't it so, Thomas?'

Thomas nodded, but added nothing to the conversation. He knew, as Agnes seemed not to, that the old man was working on more than making good the body and machinery of Gospels as it stood. He was locked into the barn at all hours, creeping through the kitchen at midnight after only two or three hours' rest, supposing Thomas to be soundly sleeping. Sounds of planing and tapping and sawing went on until dawn. And when Thomas himself slid into the barn one early morning after his grandfather had left, he found the place littered with the implements and materials of sail making – and there were two new sweeps made – different, as he saw at once, worked out to some freakish plan of the miller's own devising. The sail stocks were unusually tapering; the sails would be narrower and finer than the old ones, that was plain. What was plainer still was that though they might be fractionally smaller they would be more numerous. The old man had begun work on a new poll-end, the heavy box that carried the windshaft at its back, the sails slotted into position. This poll-end, instead of being four-square was now six-slotted. Thomas looked at it with dread, for what was needed was a whole new windshaft. His grandfather was working far beyond the capacity of a strong man of middle years – it must be his madness that made him strong, and certainly he must have lost his remaining wits. Many ingenious ropes and slings and pulleys were hung and weighted from the great beams of the enormous barn. No doubt they acted almost as well as workmates; yet the whole enterprise could only seem to Thomas more than mad, more than magical – diabolical, rather. *One for Lucifer, seen in the dark. . .* Had Gaffer Welfare summoned Satan himself to his aid?

The next day, Thomas found Lewis halfway down the track. He was sitting on the Roman milepost.

'Best not!' cried Thomas.

'Not what?'

'Sit there. The Romans left it. The Romans!'

'Aye. So Sir James did tell me.' The priest at the old palace chapel had become Lewis's tutor a week or so back. 'What of it?' He smiled in a manner Thomas found hard to bear. 'The Romans were not wizards or monsters, you know, Thomas. They were men like you and me.'

'Well – I wondered about them. And I'm still dubersome.'

'So was I – dubersome – until only yesterday!' Lewis cried, bursting into laughter. 'I believe Sir James knoweth every smallest thing that happened since the world began. He is so wise he can spare to make me wise, too – only I doubt I'm clever enough.'

Thomas was grinning now, too, though he wanted to tell Lewis about his grandfather and the trouble that was certainly brewing. 'Your head'll crack right open, Lewis Mallory, come you stuff it too full.'

'Can you read, Thomas?'

'Who'd'a learnt me? Our Betsy – she can write her name. And Saul, him she wed, he can read – so maybe she's at it b'now. Only farmers and farmers' wives, they don't have much time for such fancies. It's all ploughshares and grain, and how soon before winter to kill off the cattle.'

'You teach me to be a forester, brother, and I'll teach you to read.'

'I'll teach you, surelye,' said Thomas. 'But what'd I do wi' reading or writing? No, I thank you gratefully brother. I've no time to spare.'

'Sir James says any man may better himself – if he choose. God'll keep an eye on that man, so Sir James says.'

'What's *better?* Being a farmer's better'n being a miller's boy, that's all the better I need. And I'll get to it one day.'

'And you'll be off straight to sister Betsy,' said Lewis, who by now had heard all this a lot more than two or three times. 'And where shall I be then?'

'You'll be a forester b'then, brother.'

'I shall! I shall! So I'm to walk with you to the forest pale, and commend you to heaven, and see you on your way?'

'I must ride. The farm's far from here – even beyond Lunnon.' He looked quickly at Lewis and spoke while he had the courage. 'Maybe Master Orlebar might lend me some old horse one day?'

'*Some old horse?* There's none such at Ghylls Hatch. There's no single horse there would ever be loaned out, Thomas Welfare. And if there were – I'd see you got none.'

'That's brotherly!'

'Aye – it is!' Lewis cried hotly, his face reddening in anger. 'And you swore to be my brother. So choose, then. Brother or sister – which?'

'Nor one nor t'other – not while my gaffer draws breath,' Thomas replied, half sullen at finding himself trapped, half warmed that Lewis would try to keep him within reach. 'So,' he said, 'let be how'twill.'

The bluster had already gone out of Lewis. But the words had been spoken and remained hanging in the air between them – the threat, the choice; the decision that must surely one day be faced. *Let be how' twill*, Thomas had said. But when the time came – how might it be?

6. Forest Ways

Thomas watched Lewis grooming Solitaire while Peter Crutten kept up a flow of contradictory instruction.

'Rub harder, there. Have a care o' that fetlock! That's tender over the joint. Now – see you niver get him huffed. Grooming's to be firm, not slummocky – but he know to be sharp wi' you come you blunder and rough him.'

Thomas thought Lewis handled Solitaire to perfection so he found Peter's strictures tiresome. A horse, Thomas believed, was clean or it was dirty. Solitaire had been dirty, for he had been ridden out in torrential rain which, that past week, had turned the forest to a sudden swamp; Solitaire, under Lewis's ministration, was now clean. It seemed simple enough. But Peter Crutten, having been charged to instruct, was unlikely to skimp the matter – by the time he let Lewis go Solitaire looked fit to carry a king.

'Now come to the saddler with me,' Lewis said to Thomas. 'Old Awcock's got the work going.'

'He take his time, Old Awcock do,' said Thomas.

'He's more to do than build me a prettier saddle than any ever made!'

Old Awcock was in fact a man in his prime, but it was necessary to distinguish him from his eldest son, who had come to work at Ghylls Hatch as no doubt the other five would do in time. His workplace was full to bursting with saddles half made, saddles under repair, saddles past repair; saddles all of wood, made stout enough to carry a man in full armour, saddles ornamented and carved, saddles of Old Awcock's own design and making, built almost entirely of leather. These last hung from hooks and racks and brackets, along with harness of all kinds, looped and slung. Above the small furnace that served both to warm the place in winter and to work metal, stirrups and bits and spurs of different sizes and pattern were hung against the wall. They were often all that remained of some great horse of the past, many of which over the long troubling years of conflict between York and Lancaster – and such times were not yet done with – had been taken illegally from their owners and breeders, rounded up and driven away to death on some civil battlefield. During the middle years of the century, after the battles of St Albans and Mortimer's Cross and Towton, the whole breeding line so patiently built up at Ghylls Hatch had been threatened with extinction. Roger Orlebar's father had been alive then, and the threat and despair of it all had killed him, though he was quite a young man. . .

The saddlery stank of sweat and of leather rotted by sweat; it smelt, too, of newly tanned leather and hot beeswax. In fact the saddler was busy about waxing twine when the boys came in. He would not be turned from the task, the wax being exactly so, even for his master's young kinsman.

'It's there,' said Lewis quietly, nudging Thomas and nodding to the saddle on a stand by the far wall.

They picked their way across the uneven, littered floor and stood side by side considering the saddle. The work had certainly not proceeded very far. With the weather so slabby, Old Awcock had explained some days past, he had been kept on the go with humdrum matters. 'I'll not be content to slam the job, young Master,' he had said; meaning he would not hurry and spoil it, but rather wait for leisure to do his finest work. The saddle was to be all of leather, shaped and soft for Solitaire's satiny back. At present the leather, though shaped, lay flat, the moulding and the padding and the skilful building had barely been worked out. Unpolished, a few stitching lines lightly scored, darkly marked by the saddler's greasy hands, the leather was so well and carefully chosen that its quality was plain even to a casual eye.

'He asked should he tool it over,' Lewis said, almost in a whisper, and that a very respectful one. 'So we have said it shall have a design of laurel leaves. The laurel's an emblem of my family. It's as much mine as another's,' he added, entirely without bitterness, as if he had indeed, as he had sworn to do, forgotten all his life till now. 'Think how fine it shall look, Thomas!'

Thomas stared at the unadorned leather and tried to

imagine how it would finally be – ornamented, polished, both workmanlike and beautiful – but he could see it only as it now was. A feeling of bafflement, almost of rage, made him scowl. He looked sideways at Lewis and knew that for him the picture was entire. But he could not see that behind Lewis's rapt expression was the vision of the saddle, firm and inviting on Solitaire's strong back, of himself mounting, settling, gathering the reins, wheeling off through the high new gateway of the stable approach, riding straight-spined through bright sunshine to whatever place about the forest he might choose – to Dame Elizabeth's great house, or Gospels Mill, or to Clinkerbank where the new mill was building, or up to visit his tutor, at the chapel by the ruins, or down to Staglye village to the church there, or to any half a dozen places on errands for poor scarcey-witted cousin Jenufer Orlebar. . .

Thomas saw in Lewis's face how much was happening in his thoughts, but he could not shape or colour it. So he was filled with the desire to stamp and hammer, as if against a door that would not open for him. It was a door that might never open, since it led to a storehouse whose treasures he was not trained to recognize, whose skills could never be his, as, by birth and good fortune, they were Lewis's.

Out of doors, when they left the saddlery, the sun of Lewis's imagination was hotly shining. It was now mid-August. The recent relentless wet weather had set back the harvest plans, but a few days like this one would dry out the fields. When that happened there would be an end to carefree running about the forest for Thomas.

'Come up Clinkerbank,' he said now. 'Time I see how that mill goes on.'

'It goes well,' Lewis answered. 'I saw for myself a week ago and more.' He looked anxiously at Thomas. 'Shall there be enough milling hereabouts for two?'

'So Gaffer tell. But Gaffer's mad as ten brown hare. Seems me there'll not be work to go round.'

'What then?'

'Agnes and Miles Hoad'll get wed. Gaffer must find his place wi' them.'

'There's you, too,' said Lewis, after a pause.

'Oh aye, surelye – there's Thomas Welfare!' cried Thomas.

He gave a sudden shout and butted Lewis violently, so that he toppled and hung struggling to recover himself on the lip of the bank which ran here quite steeply. At the last, Lewis managed to grab Thomas as he began to slide, and they both ended up in the brambles below, scratched and torn and furious, hitting and pummelling, fierce as two sworn enemies.

'Adder!' yelled Lewis, making it sound so like *Arder!* which was what any forester would say, that Thomas sprang away in flight from the danger. Lewis jeered and bellowed, and continued to mock even after Thomas had knocked him down. After that they fought seriously for five or ten minutes, quite silent save for pants and snarls, rolling from the bank into the soft clearing, thrashing and snorting through the bracken like a couple of wild boars, battering down the undergrowth. Lewis was getting the upper hand, so Thomas's fury was increasing, when a hand fell on Lewis and he was yanked clear of Thomas, who struggled angrily to his feet.

'Miles. . .'

'Make an end, the pair on you,' Miles said very quietly. 'Catch young Thomas, Peter.'

'You give over, Peter Crutten! Let me be!' cried Thomas, struggling and striking out. 'I done you no harm!'

'Hold your gab, Thomas,' said Miles. 'Peter and me've got forest business to get about.'

Both men were armed and Peter had a coil of rope over his shoulder.

'*Poaching*, Master Ranger?' mocked Thomas.

'Stalking,' Miles answered, looking grim. 'And the last hour's work run into the ground, thanks to you larking grummuts.'

'Miles don't mean to say you'm a larking grummut, Master Lewis,' said Peter quickly. 'He mean young Thomas, only. No way to speak of Master Orlebar's kinsman, Miles.'

'Let'm not act the grummut, then,' said Miles, unmoved.

Thomas grinned at Lewis's face, half dignified and half gleeful. The fight was well and truly over. It need never have taken place, only Thomas, for the first time, had found himself unable to answer, when Lewis asked what should become of him if Gospels failed, *I'll go to Betsy.* . .

'We'll come along with you,' Lewis was saying eagerly.

'Two's one too many,' Miles answered, in spite of Peter's frown. 'Four's plain dunch.'

Miles was carrying the crossbow he always used for hunting. It was a fine weapon, the steel burnished. Miles had had it from his grandfather, who claimed it had been carried on a Crusade – though he had not been able to say how, if this were so, the weapon had ever reached the forest. The smith at Staglye, a very skilful man, forged the quarrels that were the crossbow's ammunition. Peter's bow was a longbow and his arrows were very finely feathered.

'Where're you bound, then, Miles?' Thomas asked, recovering his temper. 'Stalking, say you? What quarry, then?'

'The old red stag – you know'm, Thomas, he come round the mill time and agen. Best he go now. That wound he took's festering badly. Leave'm and he'll die in the bushes and we'll lose hide and horn. Be off home, then, and let Peter and me get to our work.'

Lewis opened his mouth to protest, but Thomas nudged him and he fell silent. They stood together watching the men move off through the trees.

'I'm going after,' Lewis said. 'Shall you come?'

Thomas hesitated. He wanted to follow, he wanted anyway to please Lewis, but his forester's instinct taught him that they should not go. It could in any case take Miles and Peter all day till dark and still they might not make a kill. Miles had been right when he said two was really one too many for the job. It needed good forestry and silent stalking through territory which could crack and rustle at less than a footfall, almost at a breath. Lewis was totally unskilled and Thomas himself a mere child in experience, compared with such as Miles and his cousin.

'Do as you please,' said Lewis, swift to resent the other boy's hesitation, which was long because Thomas thought slowly and carefully. And he was off before Thomas could explain or protest. Inevitably, then, Thomas in his turn followed after. When he caught up he took the lead. He knew which of the deer-runs about here the men were most likely to follow, and he led Lewis along a higher track, barely marked and much obstructed.

After a time, Thomas reached back, grabbed Lewis's wrist and stayed him. Without speaking, he moved his head to direct Lewis's attention forward and downward.

In the clearing below them, the old red stag was now resting. He carried the twelve-branched antlers of a hart royal, but he carried them low. His head hung, and the hide hung on his sick body. Long ropes of saliva fell from his jaw that was slack and showed his yellow teeth. The whole of one shoulder, from the withers almost as low as the breast, was an open, running wound, black with flies. He was not alone in the clearing. A second stag, younger, less grandly antlered but in glorious condition, proud and clean, grazed near by. As the boys peered down, he lifted his head and stood at gaze. He moved slightly into the wind, hesitated, then returned to feeding. On the far side of the clearing, Thomas saw the bracken stir and shift as if a breeze passed over it. Miles and Peter were crouching there.

Thomas breathed in Lewis's ear, 'Watch yonder.'

Again the younger animal raised his head. This time his reaction was swift. He began to move off down the trail from the clearing, then pausing to look back, stamped and tossed his antlers. He returned, circling and chivvying the sick hart, until he rose stiffly and moved away from the clearing.

Miles's crossbow had already been stealthily raised, but now it was set down.

'He need a clear view to the shoulder,' Thomas said. 'He dursn't injure the other beast, though he be Ranger.'

'Then – what now?'

'They'll get after'm quick and quiet as meece.'

Miles and Peter emerged, then, and set off silently after the deer. Because of his injury and wretched condition the old hart would move slowly, but the younger, with his harrying and hampering, was a problem.

Sidling and creeping, still on their own higher level, the two boys went after the men as the men had gone after the deer. A useful exercise in forestry for Lewis Mallory, Thomas might have thought; but he was too intent on the matter in hand. It was very warm and still, the heart of the summer afternoon. As they went the flies tormented them, but when Lewis slapped at them Thomas frowned furiously and shook his head. Did he want to rouse the whole forest by such movements? A slight breeze touched the tops of the trees, but could not cool the boys as they crawled and stooped over ground rich with the untouched harvest of years, leaves, acorns, beechmast, so rotted and dark and scented that they crumbled still further at a touch. It was a layering of decay that constantly fed and re-fuelled new life, for the seedlings sprang thick in such wealth, the brambles tore lustily as their long sturdy trailers were set aside, thick in the fringes of clearings where the sun struck through to them, the fruit already swollen and darkening, ripening towards the end of summer.

'There. . .' Thomas said, time and again, as the hot day shifted from afternoon to evening's beginnings. 'There! Now!'

But always as the bow came level with the vital spot, the younger beast, smelling danger, nosed away his companion, shifting him from clearing to clearing, moving to and fro about him and round, ever obstructing the stalker's view, and, as it seemed, protecting and shielding the elder.

'They are brothers, Thomas.'

'Maybe.' Antlers varied greatly from beast to beast, but these two had the similarity that foresters knew could mark a given strain. 'Aye,' Thomas agreed. 'I do

bluv so. They are two brothers, anyways, as we are
brothers.'

The sun grew low and the light changed. Thomas
should have been back home by now, but he did not
think of it. He was absorbed in the day's drama that
must have its bitter ending, or else be all to do again
another day. Thomas moved through the forest with
Lewis, and the forest carried on its business about them.
The birds sang on as the shadows increased, small beasts
paused in their tracks, unseen, to wait until danger went
by. Lewis and Thomas were midge-bitten, bramble-
torn. Lewis had a great tear in one sleeve and he had

ripped the knees out of his hose; Thomas was stained green with lichen from slithering under close hung branches. Neither could have given up now, unless darkness came utterly to end the chase.

When the sun dipped, a first dark shot upward from the earth. A whole new movement began about the forest. Many creatures set out on their own necessary hunting. Strings of fallow deer, abandoning the day's secrecy, moved through the high brakes, above which only their heads could be seen, and then only those of the tallest. The birdsong became a frenzy of effort before the final silence came down.

Quite suddenly, perhaps growing tired, perhaps by now over-confident, Lewis moved too quickly and came without warning on a clearing that opened at his feet. He grabbed at Thomas to save himself rolling down the bank into the open, stepped back too sharply and fell, dragging Thomas with him.

The noise was not so very great but it set the whole forest in a panic. Jays shrieked and rocketed through the branches, blackbirds chattered and many small birds let out their tiny cries which, all together, beat upon the silence that had gone before.

In the fragment of time before it happened, Thomas had seen the two stags in the clearing. So now, as they fell and the noise broke out, he saw the younger stag, at last seeking his own safety, spring away and bound towards the trail on which Lewis and he tumbled and struggled to right themselves. He shouted, shoved

Lewis's head down and fell awkwardly across his shoulders as he flung up his arms to protect his own head. The deer rose in a huge, soaring leap that carried him off into the underwood, clearing the boys by a fine span. The speed of his passing raised the hair on both their heads. At the same instant the quarrel twanged and whined from Miles's bow. The old stag, bewildered and weary, deserted at last, blundered helplessly in his sickness and his pain, then fell. His great neck that had been so powerful was flung back in one spasm. Then his head fell forward, his throat was stretched against the earth, and his antlers, as he pitched finally sideways were driven into the ground. The blood ran. Without so much as a final shudder, he closed his bleared eyes.

Miles and Peter broke cover instantly and ran to the fallen beast. Peter took out his knife and slit the animal's throat, as if to make certain he would not rise again. Miles remained looking at the two boys in a manner that added to their already shamefaced appearance. Besides all the rest, there had been a moment of considerable fear when the deer leapt towards them, and Lewis at least was still pale from the shock.

'Fair dues, Thomas,' said Miles, smiling a little, though a shade grimly, 'I do misremember any other time when four stalking did better than two in the end.'

Miles and Peter were left to deal with the stag's carcase, while the boys went on their way. Chance had brought them to the wooded ground below and around

Morphew's Mill, that stood out aggressively against the skyline of Clinkerbank. As they came up through the trees towards the spot where the felling had taken place, so they came out of twilight into an evening gilded and flushed by a lingering sunset. It was very quiet, very still. Then there came on that stillness the sound of men working – talking together, calling out orders, steadying here, thrusting forward there, heaving and straining.

'Sweeps going up,' said Thomas; and he began running forward, leaving Lewis to follow as he pleased. At a line of scrub on the edge of the big clearing, Thomas crouched down to watch.

Men were working on the mill, which stood tall and fine, bigger than Gospels, stronger because newer – as new as any new generation thrusting out the old. Thomas gasped at he looked at it, knowing that the worst must come now to Gospels. They had two sails up and were getting ropes ready to hoist the next. With the eye of one who had grown up with such things, Thomas saw how bravely the sails were built, of what excellent materials and with what fine craftsmanship. That struck him hardest of all, for just as he had grown up to understand about milling, so he had grown up in the belief that no other miller could compare with Gaffer Welfare. . . Without forewarning of disillusionment, he saw that this was not so. For younger men had come to the trade who in the meantime had learnt more – more about crafting the monster, more about how the winds might best be made to take her – men with greater power to their bodies than the old miller at Gospels could ever again command. As Thomas watched the next sail hoisted by Dan Morphew, with all his four sons down to the littlest, and neighbours making up the number, with wives and children clustered about to enjoy the triumph of the last act in the mill's making, he realized how puny were the attempts he had seen in the big barn at home. He had thought those sails so finely wrought as to have had the aid of demons, but now he knew the old man had been able to handle them only because they were so frail.

Lewis had come up now, but Thomas could not turn. His eyes had filled with terrible, with shameful tears and he did not know how to be rid of them. He heard the shouts and cries of those about the mill, but he could barely see the women running from the mill house with mugs of ale for those who were striving so well.

'Shall you tell him?' Lewis asked, his voice very low. 'Better not, I'd say. Don't tell him. Don't tell your grandfather what you've seen, Thomas. He's an old man – he's so old. Won't it break his heart?'

Thomas could not answer, he could not speak. Now the tears had spurted out, his face was red, he needed to open his mouth and cry in the shouting bawling way of a baby.

'Come on,' Lewis said, tugging at his arm. 'Come away now. Stop grieving, brother – stop grieving. I had my fill of tears three months past, and that's never to be thought of again – but I'll be weeping with you soon.'

He put his arm about Thomas's shoulder and urged him away, dragging at him until he stumbled to his feet and began to head for the path that would carry them to the home track. Even in his misery, Thomas thought of the injured deer and his anxious partner who had chivvied him away to a safer place. His tears checked and at last dried. When they came to the turn in the track, leading south to Gospels, north-west to Ghylls Hatch, Thomas went fast on his way without speaking. He knew that Lewis stood looking after him, anxious, a shade forlorn. But pride would not let Thomas turn his smeared face to give a sign of farewell or gratitude. By the time he relented, halfway to the mill, Lewis was out of sight.

When Thomas reached home there was immediately work to do, grumbles to face – where had he been so long? who did he think had done his work? wasn't he old enough to labour a full day for his keep? He flung away and set about the ordinary evening tasks of fetching water, shutting up the goose, milking the goat – which Agnes might have done, he considered. He did not speak even to her of what he had seen on Clinkerbank. That night he lay awake, hour after hour as never in all his life before. He was bitterly tired. His whole body ached with the day of scrambling up and down. His mind ached more. He did not know what would happen because he was not able to search so far. He only knew that life as he had known it might be about to end.

There was light in the sky by four o'clock. The

rooster penned in the mill yard raised his voice and another answered. The cry went on across the forest, as if it were thrown and caught and thrown again. The sound would continue, long after Thomas's ears were defeated, a sleepy sound at first, then increasingly vigorous, then strident and full of arrogance in the certainties of the new day.

A little after cockcrow, Thomas heard his grandfather coming down the stairs from above. As so often before, he went stealthily across the kitchen and let himself out into the morning. Now he was crossing the yard, now pulling the barn door just enough to slide inside. . . The old man would need the assistance of Satan himself to get free of disaster now. And if the Devil seemed far away, Thomas thought wearily that God seemed even farther.

7. 'One for Lucifer, seen in the dark . . .'

Strange weather settled over that south-eastern country-side. The sun hung round and red behind flat thin cloud. The ground threw up a mist of its own and nothing dried out. The harvest, too, delayed already by those earlier long days of rain, stayed dank and lost its strength, the stalk leaning slightly, a hint of mildew on the ear. Men watched the weather in silence, since to speak of it seemed to give it too much reality. On Sunday at church in Staglye they prayed for the harvest ardently and urgently, but still they did not say aloud that it could fail. That Sunday was the heaviest and sweatiest yet. Thomas, in his only good jerkin, panted and huffed home to Gospels with Agnes, who had had some difficulty in chasing him the long way there, in the first place. 'You'll be resting on your knees soon enough,' she had said then, when he moaned at the heat that seemed to increase with every step.

Miles Hoad was walking home with them and it was he who spoke at last about the harvest and what might happen.

'A bad time for all-us,' he said. 'No grain in the barn mean no flour in the sack. Worst of all, then, for millers.'

'We must trust in God,' said Agnes, for that was what she always did. If God were not listening and her prayer went unanswered, she made loving excuses – other matters more urgent, other supplicants more worthy, other prayers better made. . .

'The old man come near the end of his working days, Agnes. A bad harvest'd show him so. We'd be wed the sooner.'

'And am I to pray for a bad harvest? A fine start to life as husband and wife – getting happy through others' misery!'

Miles smiled a little, she sounded so sharp. He winked at Thomas, stodging along in the heavy heat.

'Your sister do ever set on to humble me,' he said, in a whisper loud enough to be heard right back at Staglye.

Thomas grinned at him. Miles was not set-up enough to need humbling, and he was far too simple and kind at heart to deserve Agnes's rebuke. All he had shown by his remark was how much he loved her and needed her.

'Gaffer'll work on till the last grain's ground, Miles,' said Thomas. 'He'll never give up otherly.'

But as he spoke he wondered if already the last grain had been ground at Gospels. He thought uneasily of Dan Morphew, who had been in church with his wife and his sons, and had seemed to pray louder than any when the priest petitioned for the harvest. The new mill had not been spoken of at Gospels since the day Jonas Turnberry brought the first news of it – not openly, that was. But it must be spoken of soon, for everyone else was talking about it, it was the present wonder of the forest all about. Thomas puzzled over whether he should tell Miles of what was in the making in the big barn. He had not told Agnes. Since she seldom had occasion to go into the barn, and even if she did might not fully recognize what was afoot, it was unlikely she would have found out for herself. The sight of the new mill, with men and boys swarming all over it as they hoisted the sails, had filled Thomas with a hot loyalty towards his grandfather. He longed to spare him, dreading what might come next. Agnes would have been horrified to know that he had even found himself praying that some disaster might come to the new mill, removing it altogether and leaving Gospels once again unrivalled. That was a sinful thing to do, and it sat uneasily on his soul. What if the prayer were somehow misinterpreted and disaster came instead to Gospels? He needed to confess the sin and get shriven – he had confessed it to Lewis and knew too well that he had been shocked. The words of his wicked request ran and ran in Thomas's mind: 'Let there be but one mill again, good Lord. . .' He had never so desparately wished words unspoken. . .

There was a cart and horse on the plat and they saw it as they came up the last steep incline towards home. The cart was filled up with bales and packs and the old horse was stretching her neck to drink at the pond.

'Jonas!' cried Agnes. 'And on a Sunday! That mean a bit more'n bread and cold bacon!'

'News of your sister, maybe,' Miles said.

'Nay – not this time. He'll be on his way back, all through from Kent.'

They had barely recognized who was visiting when they heard furious voices. Agnes began to hurry, Miles followed. Only Thomas lagged. His heart had dropped like a stone. He found himself shivering on that stifling day. The certainty came out of nowhere, strong and terrible, that trouble had shifted nearer. That whatever had to happen next had already begun. . .

'Where you bin doddling to?' his grandfather shouted as Thomas came level. 'Work to do, and fast about it. Strip that fine jerkin offn' you – and you, too, Miles Hoad – and get your hands dirtied up. Work to do, I'm saying. Agnes – you run fetch Robert Hoad here – y'r father's home, eh Miles?'

'Surelye. But he won't come working about the mill of a Sunday, Gaffer Welfare. Not even for'n old friend.'

'For shame, grandfather,' Agnes said. 'Get you in to your good dinner. There's only a dumpling or two must be thrown in the pot. Food'll be on the board soon's as you can turnabout.'

'Sunday, Monday, One day, None day!' the old man shouted. 'Work won't niver wait – as the good Lord himself knew when he told of the ox and the ass fall'n in the pit.'

'What come to him, Jonas?' Miles asked the pedlar.

'News – that's what come to'm. How could I tell that the talk's all over every part o' the forest save here?

98

He comes the last man living to know Dan Morphew set up twin stones in the new mill. That mean twice as much and twice as quick.'

'Get on your way!' cried Agnes. 'Shame on you to come taunting and flouting! Go on your way – and never a bite you'll ask for here. Get to the new mill, higgler, and see what good fare they'll spare you.'

'It's not Jonas built the mill, Agnes,' Miles said.

'Stop nabbling and nagging!' old Welfare yelled. 'Set about the sweeps! We'm to have them every one changed 'fore the next good breeze come blowing.'

Jonas had never gained such fine effect with any bit of news before – unless it might be the time he had come to tell of twelve dead of plague in the nearest town. He was uneasy at the sight of the old man's wildness – as if he might drop dead or run altogether mad at any moment.

'I never thought to see him so put-about,' he muttered.

'Best humour him,' said Miles. He began to unlace his jerkin – but then he pulled the lace tight again. 'Agnes is right, gaffer – we'll get our good dinner down us, first thing.'

'Aye – never let my cooking get spilt, grandfather,' Agnes urged, quickly joining in. 'No man work well wi' an empty belly. Come in Jonas.'

In this way they did hold the miller in check long enough for the meal to be eaten. Good as it was, the very instant the old man had wiped bread round his empty platter he was up on his feet and harrying them all to get outside. He had something to show, he insisted. He plagued Miles to come with him to the big barn. 'I set it all out there. Come quick'n you'll see for certain what's to do.'

'*Now*, gaffer?'

'Aye, now – now! We mun change they sweeps, Miles Hoad. We mun change'm this half day left.'

As Miles rose he looked at Thomas, still sitting with his mouth full. Agnes was looking at him, too. The food in Thomas's mouth became tasteless, he chewed at it as if at leather or bones. He could not swallow because there was already something else in his throat – not only fear, but the sudden understanding that he, of them all, was the one who knew the old man well enough to speak his strange language. He was the miller's boy. He and the miller and the mill all worked as one. He looked away from Miles and from his sister, concentrating on his empty platter. He had told Lewis he would be at the fishing pool between Ghylls Hatch and Mantlemass as soon after the dinner hour as he could manage.

Thomas glanced up at the door as if he planned to make a dash for it. But Jonas Turnberry, a tall man who had to duck his head to go indoors, was standing there. He had been looking after the old man, but now he turned back into the room, and his gaze, too, came to rest on Thomas.

Thomas kicked back his stool, sending it over with a resentful thud, and shoved past Jonas at the door. The miller was hauling at the high barn doors, swinging them right back so that whatever was inside could be moved easily.

'Miles! Jonas! Leave slirruping ale and come as I bid.'

He bellowed it out. His eyes were like the eyes of a bird, hard, bright and unblinking. His hair and whiskers curiously bristled. A small, bent man, he seemed now to display openly that strange energy that Thomas had felt must come from Hell itself. It was as if lightning played about him.

'Gaffer,' cried Thomas, 'bide till tomorrer. Good work never got done on a resting day.'

'Tell Miles fetch his father,' was all the old man answered. And he shouted once again, 'Fetch thy father, Miles Hoad! Fetch Robert Hoad here. He ever were a good sail-man – a strong hand wi' a rope.' And standing there in the barn doorway with his precious invention waiting inside, he began to laugh, and to sing out,

> Hoad, Hoad, hurry along –
> Help thy neighbour, right or wrong.
> Down wi' Matthew, down wi' Mark,
> Up wi' Lucifer, seen in the dark!'

'What's he saying?' Miles asked Thomas.

'He's set-on to make Gospels a six-sailer. There's three sweeps built a-ready – maybe more. In the barn...'

'Who worked with him – you?'

'None. Who, hereabouts, 'd work wi' Gaffer Welfare?'

'He built 'em alone?'

'Poor, puny, pathery things,' Thomas said. 'Like himself.'

'Best he be humoured,' Agnes said quietly, 'Get off to your father, Miles – but stay when you get home. Jonas – be on your way. Wi' none but Thomas and me to give a hand there's naun he can do.'

'Leave you? Wi' him half out of his wits?'

'There'll be no harm. But tell your father – and come when you may in the morning. Get off now, 'fore he get more wild.'

Miles glanced uneasily at Thomas. 'Aye – go,' said Thomas – then turned at once to his grandfather – 'Miles'll go fetch his father, gaffer. But you rest easy come the time he get here.'

'And tell thy cousin, Peter Crutten, I'm waiting on him,' old Welfare shouted at Miles. 'Six men, I need. One man, one sail. Thomas and Agnes make up to one man. . . That's you, me, Robert, Peter – still one short. Jonas! Where's Jonas?'

'Gone on his way,' said Agnes calmly. 'Come indoors now, grandfather.'

His answer was to turn his back on them and stump into the barn. He dragged the door behind him. In the silence that followed, they heard him singing.

'Go on now,' Agnes said to Miles. 'Maybe he'll forget, once you're gone. In the morning, bring the priest from Staglye, as well as the others. We need a man can reason wi' my grandfather.'

'I'll bring my father and Peter. As for the priest – '

'Best not,' said Thomas quickly, remembering Lucifer, Beelzebub, and his grandfather's contempt for Godly matters.

Miles went away, reluctant, troubled at leaving them. Thomas watched him go, wishing he had had the sense to send a message for Lewis, in case Miles did decide to go to Ghylls Hatch for Peter at once, rather than in the morning.

The old man remained hidden in the barn and from time to time there were sounds of hammering. It seemed best to let him alone for as long as possible. The after-noon went over as other sabbath afternoons in summer, only never so heavily and breathlessly, both within and without. Agnes sat with idle hands or paced up and down outside the house – or went tiptoe to listen at the barn door.

At last the miller opened the barn doors, setting them again as wide as they would go. He appeared, then, drag-ging one of his own new sails, pulling it with ropes like harness about his chest and shoulders. He laid it in the open and returned for a second. Again Thomas felt the old man was inspired by demons, who were helping him to use up all at one time the power remaining in his old body. He seemed like a man who spends a fortune as he lies dying. For surely by morning, when Miles came again, bringing whatever help he could, there would be nothing left of the miller but a worn-out husk.

In his concentrated frenzy of activity old Welfare remained – in and out of the mill, scrambling up the

steps, swinging himself like an agile boy about the face of the structure, trailing and fixing ropes, leaning from the topmost vent to adjust and settle the knots he had made. His skill seemed boundless. Alone, by cunning with the ropes, he had the two sails, Mark and Luke, shifted in the poll-head, waiting to be lowered.

Every now and again Thomas groaned and said he must either go to help or else try to wheedle the old man to give up and come indoors. Each time, Agnes checked him.

'He'll tire. Leave him. He'll not go on for ever.'

'He'll drop down dead, sister!'

'Leave him be,' said Agnes.

That day darkened early, belying its summer date, shutting in with a hint of mist that lightly veiled the hill, the mill house, the mill itself. The sky hung low and lower. Along the horizon a tawny flush barely supported the unbroken grey. Yet it seemed to thrust upward, as if a stronger power attempted to gain command – as if a fiery dragon lay in waiting, and the mist about the house and the mill was its dreadful breath.

Agnes, standing by the open door, lifted her head and sniffed the air.

'A change coming, Tomkin,' she said.

She slid her arm round him and drew him close. She had never called him *Tomkin* before and seldom used that soft warm voice that was more like their sister Betsy's.

For a second Thomas stood rigid in the circle of

Agnes's arm, her unusual softness making him shy. Then he felt her shaking slightly and knew she was afraid. He had to help her if he could. But he was afraid, too.

When the dark finally came, the old man suddenly appeared on the steps of the mill, sat down and put his head in his hands. None had come to help and the work was far unfinished, but his rage was spent with his bodily energy. He came indoors, stumbled up the stairs without stopping for bite or sup, and fell on to his bed. He slept at once, breathing with great snores that seemed to fill the house.

Agnes and Thomas went to bed. Thomas lay long awake and he knew that Agnes was awake, too, for more than once he heard her moving and knew that she stood listening at the stairhead. Beyond the window across from Thomas's bed the blackness was intense, thick. Only in the final second before he slid at last into a deep sleep, there was a far flash of lightning. . .

He woke with Agnes tugging and shaking him, the room now mysteriously light.

'Get up! Get up!'

He shuddered awake. 'Agnes. . .? Where is he? What come to us?'

'A great storm come. Listen. . .'

He heard the wind rolling towards them from afar, like a huge chariot with wheels the size of mill-sweeps and heavy as a hundred millstones. Ahead of the wind, standing against it and holding it briefly as it pounded forward, was the thunder, struggling and threatening.

'Where's Gaffer?' cried Thomas, pulling on his shirt.

'He run out ahead.'

'Not to the mill! He never dare go to the mill! Not in a great storm wi' lightning!'

'Hush,' said Agnes, trying to calm them both. 'Gospels weathered many storms.'

'This storm come out of hell!'

As he spoke, the sky lit up and everything in the room showed clear. The wind had rent the cloud apart that had hung over them so long. In enormous torn billows the sky churned and tumbled, pounded by the wind, knifed through by the lightning, piling up mountain upon mountain, as if the distant downs had been tossed into the air and been blown into bursting, changing shapes. They seemed, those bloated advancing monsters, like nightmare steeds ridden by dark angels, and it was they who dragged the giant chariot of wind and thunder.

Terror so filled and gripped Thomas that he could not move from the doorway, but stared and cringed and did not know which way to turn. Like any frightened animal, if he had had a hole or nest or burrow he would have hurled himself into it. All he could do was fling his arms over his head and crouch down, trying to cover both eyes and ears. Yet, if there had been only terror in him, he would have bolted back into the house – that was his burrow, his home where he might lie safe. But

he still strained towards the danger ahead, his grandfather's danger, and because of it he could not turn and
run, and because of it the fear eased out of him, and he
lifted his head and roused up. Pushing past Agnes, he ran
out into the mill yard, shouting at the full strength of
his lungs –

'Gaffer! Come to the house! Gaffer – Gaffer! Hark
what I say! *Where are you?*'

If the miller replied his voice was drowned by the
noise. The lightning was sharpened now, strengthened
like steel under tempering, bright and shining. High
above their heads the conflict had been joined, a mighty
clash of insuperable forces. The wind increased. The
sound of it almost drowned the thunder; the strength of
it could have hurled Thomas back against the house, if
he had not grabbed at the well-head and dropped on his
knees.

Then through the confusion and the tumult he heard
another sound, so familiar it would surely reach him
even if he were drowning under the ocean. The mill
sails were turning.

'Gaffer!' yelled Thomas.

He saw him now, for the lightning was almost
continuous. The mill stood in the very eye of the storm.
Every detail was clear as in bright sunlight. The miller
was astride the cap, dragging at the ropes he had so
laboriously set in place a few hours earlier. He must have
run to ease the brake, forgetting in his present state
that two sails had been made ready for lowering.

'Let her be!' cried Thomas, his voice shredded and dispersed by the wind, as thin and useless as a baby's cry. 'Let her be! Come down! Come down! Gaffer!'

He stumbled to his feet and began once again to struggle forward, shoving off Agnes who was now hanging on to his arm, trying to hold him back. He fought with her, furious at the delay, but just then she had arms and fingers as steely as the lightning.

'He'll fall for certain! He'll slip and fall!'

He did slip, but not for lack of his own skills, or because of age or fear or any reason from within himself. The sweeps went first, slinging out in a wide arc and crashing, first Mark, then Luke, splintering and shivering as they hit the earth, and splintering, too, a third sail of the new pattern that lay below the mill. Some separate spar, metal-tipped, perhaps, it was too difficult to see, flew after the sails and seemed to carry the lightning with it. For a second it linked the mill and the ground on which it stood. But the sting was in the tail of this terrible comet, striking the mill at its centre, cleaving it clean through its skull to its heart.

The miller was flung upward by the shock. His arms outstretched flailed against the sky and just as a few seconds earlier every detail of the mill's ancient structure had been shown item by item, so in that instant of time, far less than a second, the body of the man was shown – his hair and beard, his beetling brows, his deepset eyes, his hands, his arms, his old crooked body bent with his trade, even his spread fingers clutching at the air. Then, slowly it seemed, he fell from the milltop out in an arc as the sails had fallen, and reached the ground as they had done, crashing among their wreckage.

Above him and about him, the wind still in the two sails remaining, the sails still turning, the mill broke up as the wind tore into the rent the lightning had made. Gospels fell piece by piece apart. Timbers and spars, cogs and levers, spindles and shafts, the meal-bin the sack hoist, the grain hopper – all shivered and fell as the bodywork was shed by the machinery and the very heart of the mill lay bare. Then the windshaft slipped, declined and snapped, the last sails were shattered, the great stones fell through to the ground, carrying the crown tree with them. Within little more than minutes, as the huge wind tugged at the ruin, there remained nothing standing but the centre post and its supporting quarter bars, with the steps and the tailpole in pieces.

Thomas ran to his grandfather, lying broken among the broken bones of the mill, his love and his hate, and

as he went he knew that Miles was somewhere there, and others, even perhaps Lewis Mallory. As he went he stumbled over the wreckage and fell heavily. He cried out and tried to clasp his arm and heard the bone snap and felt it part. The pain seemed to be breathed in through his nostrils, it was so sharp and terrible.

'Brother, brother!' he heard Lewis crying, as he crouched beside him and tried to raise him up.

The movement finished Thomas for the time being.

8. Whipping Boy?

It was mid-November before Thomas's arm mended
well enough to be used properly, and even then not
without some pain – that much he did not complain of,
for he had been hampered too long and deprived of
activity. By that time a great many things had happened.
Strangest was the fact that for almost three months he
had been living at Ghylls Hatch. Master Orlebar had had
him carried there on the terrible night of the storm, and
Agnes had gone with him – wreckage from the mill had
torn open the roof of the mill-house, and she could only
go to Miles's home otherwise, a household all of men
and therefore unsuitable. At Ghylls Hatch there was
poor Jenufer Orlebar, with her jangled wits, and many
servants besides, so it was more fitting and decent that
Agnes should be housed there until she was Miles
Hoad's wife. Thus from Ghylls Hatch they set out to
bury Gaffer Welfare, and from Ghylls Hatch Agnes
went again to church and was wed to Miles. Thomas
was well enough to go to the wedding and enjoy the
feast afterwards that Master Orlebar gave them out of
his kind heart and generous hand. But he had been too
ill to go with the rest to bury the old man. It had been

his idea, though, that his grandfather's coffin should be made of wood from the mill's wreckage.

In his sickness and fever Thomas had wept and raved and shouted blame on himself for praying to God that there might be only one mill in their part of the forest; for so there was, now, but the wrong one. Lewis's tutor, Sir James, sat by his bedside and held his hand, praying with him and for him, and assuring him of God's most certain forgiveness. He had been thoughtless, not sinful, the priest told him gently – and the prayer itself had been inspired by care for his grandfather. . .

There could be no thought of Thomas's riding to Betsy while his arm was so bad, even if he had had a horse to carry him, and by the time it was better the winter was well begun.

'Now you shall stay till spring!' said Lewis, as pleased and cockahoop as if he had arranged the whole business from start to finish.

'There's Agnes. She think I best go live wi' her and Miles.'

'She'll have her own children any time, see if she doesn't.'

'She'm barely wed!' cried Thomas.

'Babes take less time than foals, Thomas Welfare, and if you go to that place you'll find yourself put out by summer.'

'Then my arm'll be good again. I'll go to Betsy. I could maybe go wi' Jonas Turnberry.'

'He won't be by for months and months more. You're bound to stay *here!*'

This conversation, beginning and ending in much the same place, occurred every few days.

Though he protested from pride and good manners, Thomas had no wish in the world to go and live with Agnes and Miles. Miles would make him into a forester, and that was a fine thing to be – but Thomas was set to be a farmer. He wanted to sow and harvest the grain he was used to seeing ground and sacked. Where Betsy lived there was some hill grazing and they kept their few sheep, and Betsy's husband had a brother who worked as a herdsman for the lord of the manor.

It had sounded quite grand when Jonas described the way Betsy and Saul lived – but living at Ghylls Hatch had given Thomas a different view. He had never eaten so well – Lewis had told him he was getting fat. He slept on a pallet bed in a corner of Lewis's own chamber – which was colder than the mill-house kitchen, certainly, with no just-breathing fire to wink an eye in the dark night, but he had twice the amount of covering. While he was so ill, his broken arm bringing a raging fever, every woman in the place had been ready to tend him, not least Jenufer, who sat beside him and sang and muttered, but always smiled at him when he woke. It was for Lewis's sake that the servants took such care of him, for everyone knew that Lewis would be master of Ghylls Hatch one day and they wished to stand well with him from the start. Thomas did not resent this, or indeed think much about it. If he had, he would have preferred to think he was cared for as Lewis's brother, the sharer of an oath so deeply sworn it was better than true kinship.

'They bin a-turning that head o' yourn,' said Peter Crutten sourly. 'You're that perked-up you'll soon dread to name your own kin.'

This was bitterly unfair and made Thomas turn crimson.

'That's scabby talk!'

'Who care what come to the miller's lad – but see how soft they use Master Lewis's whipping boy!'

'We're friends – brothers!' *Whipping-boy!* He hated Peter for using the words.

The trouble with Peter was, that his own cousin having married Thomas's sister made him distant kin himself. He felt entitled to harry Thomas. He had been working at Ghylls Hatch for Master Orlebar since he was six years old, but he knew well he would never have been taken into the household as Thomas had been. Peter was an amiable fellow in ordinary circumstances, if over-humble to his superiors. He resented Thomas's preferment and he began to count over his own grievances – how he had no indoor place but slept in the stable loft, how he had wanted Old Awcock's youngest daughter for his wife, but she was promised to a more solid man, and Roger Orlebar had upheld the parental decision in the matter. All manner of things that he had accepted as part of his lot irked and irritated Peter Crutten. He took to nagging at Thomas whenever an opportunity came his way.

Thomas had slipped into membership of the Ghylls Hatch household without any word being said. At table he sat by Lewis, and while his arm was still bad, Lewis thought nothing of stripping his meat off the bone for him. They were much together, and where Thomas had been the leader in foresty pursuits, leaping and climbing, snaring and stalking, Lewis was the one now who paused and looked back, and gave a hand where it was needed. And as Lewis began to speak more roughly and with a local turn of phrase, so Thomas found his own manners growing smoother. He was to walk more gently about the house, Master Orlebar had told him, not to batter on doors before opening them but gently scratch for admission, nor clatter on the stairs, nor bang his ale mug on the board. . . It was little enough, for the household, lacking a real mistress to give it grace, was rough and easy anyway. Thomas would have found very different manners, say, at Dame Elizabeth FitzEdmund's manor of Mantlemass. Lewis told him as much once.

'She keep quite courtly ways, I reckon. The mistress sit high and the servants sit low – in the proper way. Be thankful, brother, for the place you come to!'

They were in the stables at the time and Thomas swung his foot to bang with his heel against the wooden stall where he was leaning. It would make a good crashing boom, as he knew from experience. But he refrained, and set his foot down quietly – feeling poor-spirited but sensible.

Now the delayed winter came sweeping across the forest. The blow was from the south-east, the wickedest wind of all. Against common sense, Thomas had hoped to have word of Betsy before the weather finally broke. He should have known better than to suppose Jonas Turnberry would appear again this end of the year. He had carried Betsy the family news when the mill was destroyed and that had been the last of him. All the signs were of a hard winter. It might well be that Thomas would be unable even to reach Agnes to see how things went with her. They would be shut up, all of them, within a small compass, until spring. The cattle were being slaughtered for salting, the hogs called in from pannage in the forest – soon hocks and haunches hung smoking among the rafters. Ghylls Hatch ran no sheep save two or three for mutton and tallow, though Dame Elizabeth owned a fair flock grazed on upland country and driven straight to market; a few ewes in lamb were brought to eke out the winter at home, but these were considered by older hands than the lady of the manor to be a charge on the household rather than a benefit.

The latecoming winter meant a meat supply running on into spring, and at the first sign of snow Master Orlebar felt able to increase his household by one more. Sir James was to leave his own lodging among the cold ruins and come for shelter to Ghylls Hatch.

'He shall care for our winter souls, Lewis,' his cousin

said. 'There will be days hard and dry enough for him to return to say mass in the chapel – but others when he shall celebrate for us here.' He laughed at Lewis's face, which did seem to suggest that sanctity at close quarters and for long might prove an ordeal. 'It cannot be all prayers, boy – Sir James will be on hand even in deep weather to see to your lessons. The old shall be shriven and the young instructed! Thomas Welfare – what do you say to sharing Lewis's lessons?'

'I never did read and I never writ, sir,' said Thomas, alarmed. 'Nor I haven't the brain for it, I bluv.'

'And *I* bluv we shall soon see about that,' said Master Orlebar.

They did see. Thomas strove and Thomas wept, in utter and abysmal bewilderment. Lewis tried to laugh him out of his worry, then began to fuss that his own sworn brother was left so far behind. . .

'They'll never make a scholar out'f a miller's boy,' said Peter Crutten. 'Best you settle to be a stable lad, Thomas. There'll be a good place for you – Master Lewis'll speak out for you when you've grew a bit.'

Thomas scowled and did not answer. Peter's words turned and nagged in his mind for days. He tried not to understand what they meant – but he knew in his heart and had always known. Peter meant that they were still children, he and Lewis, and so their friendship could be smiled upon. But one day they would find they had grown out of boyhood and everything would change. Must it be *Master Lewis*, then, with Thomas ready to snatch his cap off respectfully – the red cap that Betsy had given him, that had made him proud? He would not believe it. He thought instead how Lewis had ridden with the men through that night of dreadful storm, and had crouched at his side, calling him 'Brother! Brother!' as his senses left him.

Yet the black seed was sown in Thomas's mind that the days of brotherhood could end. He hated Peter. He wished harm to him – like boils or winter ague or backache. To spite Peter by growing greater in the world of men, Thomas gritted his teeth and slaved with fresh energy at his lessons, trying to understand the strangest matters, trying to believe that letters written on paper in a particular order meant a certain spoken sound, but that one letter out of place could make another sound, and that sound just as needful to knowledge. He counted up on his fingers to see if four and six, or two and eight, or nine and one did indeed make ten. . . It was only when Sir James spoke of distant days, telling how a race of strangers had come from a distant country to govern Britain, that something shifted in his mind, like a pebble sent spinning from between the grinding stones it had clogged. The strangers were called Romans. He thought of the two mileposts on the forest – the Romans had left those behind. He understood fully for the first time that they had been men like any others. Until then he had been hearing. Now he listened.

Christmas was fine and dry, the ground hard but

not treacherous. There was no snow. Thomas was able to visit Agnes and Miles, and Lewis went with him. Lewis rode beautiful Solitaire, not yet finally and entirely called his. Solitaire was in need of a stretch, and Master Orlebar had told Peter to find Thomas a suitable mount. He had suggested Bryony, a tight little black pony with streaming tail and mane.

'You'll never hold'm, wi' that arm o' yourn,' said Peter. And saddled up scrawny, kind-hearted old Greygoose instead. She moved away with the utmost docility, while Solitaire danced and jingled his bit.

'He only thinks to care for you,' Lewis said. 'Your arm does still pain you.'

'Never,' scoffed Thomas, looking black.

In fact he was not at all certain that he could have held Bryony, short of exercise, in that crisp heady air. He knew his arm to be still unpredictable, and to say it never hurt him was absurd. Perhaps indeed Peter was being both sensible and considerate, but Thomas found him merely condescending. They rode out into thin sunshine, and Lewis nobly held in Solitaire for the sake of Greygoose, and they took some time to reach their destination.

'One day,' said Lewis, 'we'll take turns with Solitaire and ride all the way to the coast.' He burst into such laughter that he might almost have swayed out of the saddle. 'I was going to be a cabin boy! A cabin boy! Do you recall that?'

Thomas nodded, grinning. He looked at Lewis's

healthy laughing face and remembered how he had been that day – a wraith, wrung with misery, yet even in that state steadfast, refusing pity, silent, as he had been silent ever since, and ever would be, about the true cause of his arrival there among them; knowing how to be private even in despair. The change in him was so great it was as if some other lad rode with Thomas. . . And so must he himself be changing, Thomas thought in surprise, with the changed circumstances of his life. What if Agnes found him already a stranger?

She ran out when she heard them coming. Thomas threw himself out of the saddle and dashed to meet her, seizing her and hugging her, as she hugged him in return. Then she stood back with her hands on his shoulders and he realized how much taller he had grown – she was all but shorter than he was.

'Oh Thomas – Thomas Welfare! What a great spanking lad you'm come to be!'

Over his shoulder, then, she saw Lewis. Thomas felt her stiffen slightly. She smoothed down her apron. Did she just manage to check, and that uneasily, the beginnings of a bobbed curtsy? Thomas knew that it was so.

'Bid him welcome!' he said, sharp, in her ear.

But instead of crying then 'Welcome!' Agnes only said sedately, 'Good-day to you, Master Lewis.'

'And to you, Mistress Hoad,' cried Lewis, sweeping her a great bow that turned the moment happily to a joke. 'But Thomas and I are brothers, well you know,' he said. 'So, you must embrace me also, sister Agnes.'

It worked very well, it was so graceful. He sounded
like a courtier, Thomas thought, admiring. He watched
Agnes, red in the face, hold out her hands, and Lewis
kiss her robustly on each cheek.

It was not only because he had ridden laggardly
Greygoose that Thomas felt left behind.

But it was a good day. Agnes had cooked a meal as
good as any served at Ghylls Hatch, and hotter, too,

since the distance from fire to table was an eighth as great. It was a fine thing to see her and Miles comfortably together at last. Their holding was small enough, a forest ranger's perquisite which Agnes had been striving in one way and another to make better than it was. They had an acre, room at least for one cow, for goats and geese, and along the rim of their pond six white ducks lay in the cold, their heads tucked in, looking like wrung linen clouts waiting to be hung out to dry.

'And is all well, Thomas?' Agnes asked, drawing him aside when it was time to go.

He nodded. 'I'm being learnt – I'm being taught to read and write.'

'Then you'll not go to Betsy, come spring?'

'Maybe not, maybe so.'

'You must do what you see best.' She looked at him in a puzzled way, even a little sad. 'You come almost to a man, Tomkin.'

He looked sheepish, thinking she flattered, for it was only months since they parted, and he had certainly no beard to show. All the same, in the spring he'd be thirteen years old – an age at which any lad might seek his fortune, go to war, be tied 'prentice, or get sent for learning to the university. He hugged her roughly to cover his embarrassment.

'Take care, now! I bin wed since August last. God willing I'll have my first child by May.'

He looked at her for a second almost in horror. He

had been the little brother. Already, in Betsy's home, there was a Thomas younger than he. And now Agnes! His place had changed. He was thrown out. Maybe he was tied to Ghylls Hatch after all, and need never be otherly. . .

It was dark when they left, with a high bright moon that led them easily and safely home.

'Full moon two nights from now,' Lewis said. 'How if we rode to the sea by moonlight? Home before dawn and none the wiser. And you on Bryony this time, surelye!'

'There'd be trouble.'

'Why? Muffle their hooves till we're well away.'

'Peter Crutten sleep in the stable loft.'

'You're afeard!'

'No. . .'

'Get on, you silly nidget – say, Yes, or I'm bound to go alone.'

'Yes,' said Thomas.

If things went wrong, he'd be blamed for certain. Hadn't Master Orlebar, right at the start, however laughingly, said he should be Lewis's whipping-boy? Hadn't Peter said the same?

'Do you truly mean *Yes?*' asked Lewis, aware of some reserve.

'I do mean it,' Thomas said.

9. To Keep or Give Away . . .

Some times, Thomas thought, must live for ever. Like
the death of Gospels. Like the night he and Lewis
somehow sneaked out the horses without Peter or any
other discovering what was happening, and rode out in
full moonlight, and saw the sea. Lewis had seen it before,
but not Thomas. They saw it from the summit of the

downs, the moon slipping and glittering – like frost on glass, Lewis said – Thomas had not seen much glass. At the edge of the shore, Lewis told him, there were waves breaking into foam, forever sifting sand and pebbles. And he told Thomas, letting himself touch for once on times before he came to the forest, that he had sailed in a boat to France when he was very small and come safe home again. . . Unfortunately, they had taken so long about finding their way to this point that they dared not ride on to the sea's edge, but were bound to turn and make for home.

It was a holy sort of night. Deer moved freely, foxes ran and paused, looking back dartingly, one paw raised,

brush stiff and fluffed behind. The horses pricked their ears at the cry of owls. The moon swam on and over, grew huge, changed colour and began to sink. In the pause between moonset and winter sunrise the boys moved in near-darkness and wondered why they had come. All tracks seemed obstructed, brambles were fierce with old thorns, branches whipped at the riders's faces. Both horses, weary now, began to peck and stumble. They were nervy, taking their mood from their masters, both alarmed by the knowledge that they could not now get back in time to avoid being found out. At one point pausing to choose which of two equally unpromising ways, an old boar badger stodged grunting across their path. That did for Bryony, who reared up, chucked off Thomas, and went plunging among the undergrowth.

Taken unawares, Thomas landed lightly. He felt the jar to his arm, but there was nothing worse.

'I never should've thought o' this ploy,' said Lewis, helping him up. 'I caught my scarcey wits from cousin Jenufer.'

The roughness in his speech strangely comforted Thomas, levelling the pair of them and making him feel that when they reached home things might work out better than he feared.

'Catch Bryony,' was all he said.

It was a hard business, the creature being already much alarmed. He went deeper and deeper into the under-wood and by the time Lewis had headed him off and

Thomas grabbed the dragging rein, Bryony was very much torn and cut about; and there was a gash breaking one knee.

From then on the boys went in silence. The sky had clouded, the sun did not show, the last effulgence from the moon was drawn away. By the time they rode into the stable yard it was full morning. They had been missed long enough for a hue and cry to be planned. Several of the Ghylls Hatch men were saddling up in preparation. As the pair rode in, Roger Orlebar came from the house to mount and lead the hunt.

Lewis was out of the saddle first. He stood by Solitaire's head and waited for his kinsman to speak, offering no excuses. Thomas slid from Bryony's back and stood quietly, too. Instinct told him this was best left to Lewis.

'Go into the house,' Master Orlebar said to Lewis. He was very pale. Few of them had seen him angry; Thomas had never imagined such a thing. He was angry now, but it was easy to see even so that his rage was more like a terrible pain in his head.

'I persuaded Thomas to go with me,' said Lewis.

'Go inside.'

'It was my idea, cousin. Thomas had never seen the sea.'

'The sea!' He could not have supposed they had been so far. His glance shot past Lewis to the horses. His fury seemed likely to burst him. 'Get in! Do as I say. Go indoors.' He called out, sharp and hard, 'Peter Crutten!'

'Master?'

'Take your young kinsman, if you care to call him so –
and punish him – punish him for two riders and two
horses.'

Lewis shouted furiously, 'Thomas never did want to
come! I made him!'

Roger Orlebar gave him one swift hard blow across
the face, and as he staggered, caught his arm and jerked
him away. Lewis struggled wildly for a second or two,
then seemed to recover his dignity. He stalked beside his
cousin, matching his stride to avoid being dragged.

'Get you in likewise,' Peter snarled at Thomas.
'What'd I tell? The stable's your place and you'll keep
it now. Get in, I tell thee, Thomas Welfare. Now – see
what it cost to be named Master Lewis Mallory's
whipping boy!'

Thomas had taken many a beating in the past. This
time he took his own and Lewis's, telling himself that at
least Master Orlebar would not lift his hand again.
Thomas had as good as felt the blow given to Lewis, as
well as all the rest, and he lay all day in the straw in the
stall where Peter had chucked him when he tired, telling
himself he was lucky his arm had not broken a second
time. He lay face down and tears of pain and misery
soaked into the straw. Yet when they dried it was
because he had remembered the wonder of the immense
ocean and the moon painting it. Lewis and Sir James
between them had brought him to an awareness of such
things. And that made him think how much had hap-

pened to him since he and Lewis swore brotherhood that day in summer, so that he wept again. He knew in his heart it might well be ended now.

The day wore over, its sounds, familiar and unvarying, continued beyond the barred door, and Thomas grew hungry as well as miserable. It was almost dark when the bolts were drawn, and he started up and then fell back crying out in pain at the sudden movement. It was Jenufer Orlebar who came in and pulled the door behind her, moving so feather-footed it was no wonder he had not heard her approaching. She was carrying a lantern and had a basket under her cloak. Without any ado or wasteful words, she sat down in the straw beside him and uncovered the basket. There was bread and meat and a flask of small beer and Thomas took the food, even without thanks, and munched eagerly.

'My brother locked Lewis in,' said Jenufer eventually. 'Else he'd come himself wi' the food.'

She was a strange, wispy woman, sometimes so merry and sometimes full of wretchedness, sobbings and wild talk. Her hair was forever blowing about her face, uncoifed and straggling, and her dinner, so Lewis had said, was more in her lap than her mouth, so that her dress was stained and poor looking. Thomas peered over his hunk of bread and meat and saw, in the lantern light, how tenderly and softly she watched him. He thought of his mother, of Betsy, of Agnes. He dropped the welcome food and leaning towards her he put his head against her thin breast and broke into crying again.

'God bless thee,' said Jenufer, rocking him. 'Fine again tomorrer. See you, now – all pain goeth in God's good time.'

'I'll needs be gone from here now,' he said, gulping and snuffling, and feeling like anyone's silly baby. 'I'll needs leave when the weather change. Aye, it's so – it's so.'

'Lewis shall not let you.'

'He done his best – he'd've taken blame. Only the Master's kin never get beat. Better he'd stopped silent and saved himself that gentleman's blow about his face.'

'Oh dear Lord Jesu!' cried Jenufer. 'You're wise as twelve men, Thomas Welfare!'

'I speak true!'

She did not answer, only held his hand and stroked it. He had made her sad, now. Her eyes filled with tears, her fingers pulled at her lip, her face crumpled. He went back awkwardly to his eating, and she wept continuously as she watched him, so that he was almost glad to see the poor soul go.

It was true that everything changed after that night. Thomas stayed working with Peter in the stable. Peter was much softened in manner – as if having asserted his seniority he could become his better self again. It had been too much for him altogether to see such a foresty lad so set up, and growing every day nearer the master than his men.

'You'm a good lad wi' horses,' he said. 'That were

a sore mess you got poor Bryony into. But – all-ways – you'm a good lad wi' horses.'

Lewis, who had been much about the stables, still learning to care for Solitaire in a manner Peter considered acceptable, came mooning about the place more than ever now Thomas was tied to his labours. If he could sneak leave from lessons, he went straight to the stables, and it might be that Sir James saw his wretchedness and hoped to cheer him.

'Whatever they think to do,' cried Lewis, 'we're still brothers sworn. It can never be otherly. It'll be easier soon – my cousin'll surely forget, and then we'll have our time together again.'

Thomas shook his head. He was mucking out Solitaire's stall – which should by rights be Lewis's job, only he seemed to have forgotten. To show how little he cared, Thomas kept his red wool hat firm on his head, confident he would not snatch it off even for Master Roger Orlebar himself.

'Your cousin remember'mself I'm the miller's boy,' said Thomas. 'I know how it come. He think shame to've let me get that perked up.'

'I'd have taken the bannicking, you know that.'

Thomas knew this was true, but he almost wanted some way of despising Lewis, so that their parting need not seem so much like the end of a world.

'Well, then,' said Lewis, slouching against the door, his thumbs hooked in his belt, 'what next? Shall you stay forever in the stables?'

'Nay, I'll be gone.'

Lewis made no outcry. He sighed deeply and said only, 'When? How?'

'Come spring, I'll get to Betsy's.'

'How?' insisted Lewis.

'Steal a horse, maybe. Plenty to choose of.'

'You never would.'

Thomas did not answer. He never would – but he was not going to admit it.

'How?' nagged Lewis. 'How shall you set about it?'

'Leave me be,' muttered Thomas. 'Master Lewis.'

At that, Lewis turned away and went out of the stables back to the house. He moved slowly, kicking at the ground.

The rest of that season was soft. The spring showed itself early, then fled again. The softness gave way to a blackthorn winter. The cuckoo hesitated in full voice and was silent in the last of the south-east wind, blowing now untempered by the long days' sunshine, blowing itself out before it was beaten. Thomas worked on in the stables. Master Orlebar was his old friendly self, there might never have been that day when his anger broke over them. But whatever he had decided then he did not intend to change. He still encouraged Thomas, but in a different way – not to learning and lessons but to skill with the horses. In time, he had said, Thomas should have a hand in the schooling. When they rode a train of horses for sale in London, Thomas should maybe go too.

'If so,' said Thomas to Lewis, 'then I'll be on my way to Betsy's. I'll leave 'em all and plod on best's I may.'

'Well,' said Lewis, sounding relieved, 'you can rest easy till then.'

'Too long.'

'That's mannerly! Why is it too long?'

'I'll be made full servant to Ghylls Hatch, b'then. Fallen into the way of it, see you.'

'You can see into the future, then?'

'You and the rest learned me to think for myself.'

Lewis went red at that. He was angry, but he swallowed his rage because he did not want to let Thomas go.

'But we know – you and I – we know we're sworn brothers.'

'Am I to pull my forelock to my brother?'

Late March, and Jonas Turnberry passed through that countryside, and sought Thomas at Ghylls Hatch.

'Your sister Betsy's bonny and livesome. Your godson grow fast and healthy. When shall you go to her, come you promised? She say to tell you she and Saul'd dearly respect another pair of hands.'

Thomas was saddling up Solitaire for Lewis to ride out with his cousin to the weaver – Lewis was grown out of almost all the clothes he owned. Thomas, older but smaller, had been wearing them already for some time. From behind, as he slid a saddle over Solitaire – Old Awcock was still working on the promised beauty –

Thomas looked much as Lewis had looked a year ago. It was true, as he had claimed, that he had been taught to think. He thought now that he could never hold his head high until he could step out in his own clothes. . .

When it was Easter, Thomas rode with Lewis to church, but so did all the rest – and try as he would he found himself unable to ride level as he had done in the past, but hung back a little, like any groom. He knew he made Lewis angry and miserable, he was angry himself – not least because Peter smiled and nodded his approval.

It was very fine that Easter Sunday. Dame Elizabeth returned with them from Staglye, to exchange greetings with Jenufer, who had not gone to church. Master Orlebar halted his train before the house. He was smiling and contented, as men are whose souls have been made comfortable and who see the future clear.

'Wait with us, madam,' he said to Dame Elizabeth. 'I have a promise to fulfil – and shall do it now.' He snapped his fingers at one of his men, who stepped forward and handed him a roll of parchment. Everyone was smiling and expectant, most knowing what was to come. 'Now, Lewis,' his cousin said, 'this is the day I have chosen to make Solitaire truly your own. You have learnt to care for him well, as Peter Crutten tells me. . .' He turned to Dame Elizabeth, explaining, 'I would not make him full owner till he proved himself in saddle *and* stable!'

'So he has done well, then?' she said, smiling at Lewis. 'I see it must be so. Shall you learn a smith's part, too, Lewis Mallory, and get yourself to shoeing?'

If she was laughing at him, it was very kindly. Lewis, Thomas saw, was too stirred to take in anything but the fact that he had won his prize.

'Here, boy,' said his cousin, 'here on this roll I have had writ down the names of Solitaire's forebears back to his great-great-granddam. Take it and study it. Learn it. The day will come when you and I shall decide together how best to continue the line.'

He handed over the roll, and embraced Lewis, with that blend of modest affection and shyness that made him liked as much as respected.

'Sir,' stumbled Lewis, 'sir, how shall I . . . What shall I say, cousin? I do thank you for the gift. I do thank you, sir.'

'Old Awcock has a thing that is yours, too, Lewis. The saddle is done. See for yourself.'

The saddler carried forward his finished work. He had it covered with a cloth. Lewis whipped it away and showed the splendour of the thing – the leather worked and supple, oiled to softness, stitched and padded to firmness, and along its borders the tooled device of laurel leaves as he had promised.

'Change the saddles, Thomas,' Master Orlebar said.

'I shall do it!' cried Lewis.

'It is for Thomas, cousin. Thomas shall do it.'

So Thomas, his eyes on his work, deft and swift,

switched the saddles, and then insultingly offered Lewis a leg up.

As if to match him, Lewis stepped back and said to Master Orlebar, 'Let Thomas ride him.'

'Come, now, Lewis,' his cousin said. He looked troubled, for Lewis had spoilt his fresh pleasure in the occasion, and maybe he was wishing Dame Elizabeth and all the rest were not there to see the clash of wills. 'What argifying creatures lads can be!' he said to her. His heart was soft enough towards Thomas, only he thought he knew now beyond doubt what was most fitting. 'This is your own mount, Lewis Mallory, for you to care for as you have proved you know how.' He smiled, but still uneasily. 'Solitaire is for *you*, Lewis. He is not given lightly.'

'Sir, since he is mine – may I not honour a friend with skill to ride him?'

'You are a stubborn boy,' Roger Orlebar said. 'Do as you wish with what is yours.'

He turned away and gave Dame Elizabeth his arm to lead her into the house. Lewis had won, but it was a poor sort of triumph. All there were uncomfortable and somehow disappointed, and when Lewis turned to speak to Thomas, he had vanished.

He had gone to the stable and stood struggling with the now certain knowledge that he could no longer remain at Ghylls Hatch. He heard Lewis lead in Solitaire, and looking across the stable into the yard he saw him with the smoky mist of the warm spring day behind

138

him, making him look twice his breadth and height. Lewis came inside like a giant, and like a giant he spoke at once to his sworn brother:

'Take Solitaire.'

Thomas took the bridle as if to lead the horse to his own stall, but Lewis said, 'No. Take him and go to your sister.'

Thomas gasped and fumbled over his reply. 'I cannot. How should I? A gift to you from your own kin – and it mean much to him, the way you come to handle your horse.'

'Well,' said Lewis, drawing himself up, pulling in his breath as if he needed some special supply to help him speak firmly, 'I say it mean much to me, Thomas Welfare, to give where I do choose.'

Thomas stared at Lewis as if, veiled until now as the saddle had been, a new strength and goodness was disclosed. He was no longer the boy he had been, a companion to be taught country living, a clever rival for lessons with an advantage over his fellow pupil enough to cause despair. He was indeed that friend and brother he had sworn to be, offering so immense a proof of himself that Thomas saw plainly there could be no rejection. He was not persuading himself in this to his own advantage. He was, rather, realizing through his new ability to think a shade ahead, the beginning of a man's reasoning rather than a boy's, that to refuse a great gift is to cast down the giver and trample on his sacrifice.

He paused a moment longer, smiling at Lewis with so much love in his heart it was like a beacon.

'Thomas?'

'Aye?'

'Speak out! We may never meet again – never, never. But for both our pride's sake – do as I say. Better never to see my brother than to call him my lackey!'

'Aye,' said Thomas again, still gazing at Lewis, 'I have to go, surelye.'

'When?'

'Now. Else it shall be never.'

'I'll joss you up,' said Lewis, with no pause, no hesitation. 'What shall you take with you?'

'What I stand in – and that's first of all yourn.'

There was a huge rough cloak hanging behind the stable door. Lewis pulled it down and rolled it to carry at the saddle bow.

'Bread, Thomas? Drink?'

'Find as I go. A forester know how.'

'Money?'

'Earn my keep like any other.'

There seemed no more to be said. Thomas was mounted, Lewis was walking at his side, Solitaire was stepping as proudly for the miller's boy as for Master Orlebar's kinsman. It was just after noon, late to start a journey, but this journey could not be delayed. Thomas headed Solitaire up the track and Lewis ran alongside, unable to say good-bye. Over to their left, they saw a

horse and rider turning from Ghylls Hatch. Dame Elizabeth FitzEdmund was returning home to Mantlemass.
She saw them and reined in. She raised her arm, as if she
knew all there was to know about Thomas Welfare,
Lewis Mallory, the need for a boy moving on to manhood to strike his own blows.

Lewis waved back. Thomas lifted his red cap and held
it in greeting and farewell high above his head. It sped

his thoughts to Betsy. His, she had said, to keep or give away – as Master Orlebar had said of Solitaire: *Do as you wish with what is yours.*

Thomas bent from the saddle. He clapped his red cap on Lewis's head, and as he settled it there he kicked up Solitaire and bounded forward, leaving Lewis standing on the track staring after him, both hands ramming on the red cap as if it must stay there for ever after until the end of his days.

Thomas rode on fast. He was leaving the forest, going without a farewell to Agnes, without another look at what had been his home, the mill wreck still strewn about, the broken house with other faces already at the door. Ahead of him the trees parted to let in a far horizon, and there hovered a kestrel and his mate, she big and bold, he delicate, fierce, certain. Before either made a strike, Thomas would be past. The deer and the badger and all that he had known, the lark, the scutty wren, the heron widely and gracefully flapping, the swans with necks outstretched – to these he was saying good-bye. There would be others – but to these he was saying good-bye.

He glanced back. He saw Lewis still, for he had run fast to high ground. The red cap that had seemed once like a single poppy in a green field became at that moment more like a drop of blood. For a second Thomas hesitated. He would go back. He would be Lewis's servant rather than leave him, swearing allegiance as a vassal to his lord, a subject to the monarch – anything rather than quit him for ever.

But the moment passed. It would not do. The forest had bred him stubborn and he could not bend his neck. He rode on again, his teeth hard gritted. He had a long journey ahead, through country he did not know, among threats and dangers. But already he was leaning towards the end of it, when he would come wearily at the dusk of some long day to Betsy's, and shout out to her, and see her at the door.

'Tomkin! Tomkin!' she would cry.

Then he would be home.